Passport Diaries

Passport Diaries

TAMARA T. GREGORY

AMISTAD
An Imprint of HarperCollins*Publishers*

A hardcover edition of this book was published in 2005 by Amistad, an imprint of HarperCollins Publishers.

PASSPORT DIARIES. Copyright © 2005 by Tamara T. Gregory. All rights reserved. Printed in the United States of America. No part of this book may be used or reproduced in any manner whatsoever without written permission except in the case of brief quotations embodied in critical articles and reviews. For information address HarperCollins Publishers, 10 East 53rd Street, New York, NY 10022.

HarperCollins books may be purchased for educational, business, or sales promotional use. For information please write: Special Markets Department, HarperCollins Publishers, 10 East 53rd Street, New York, NY 10022.

FIRST AMISTAD PAPERBACK EDITION PUBLISHED 2006.

Designed by Stephanie Huntwork

The Library of Congress has cataloged the hardcover edition as follows:

Gregory, Tamara T.
  Passport diaries / Tamara T. Gregory.—1st ed.
    p. cm.
  ISBN-10: 0-06-078927-1
  ISBN-13: 978-0-06-078927-5
  1. African American women lawyers—Fiction.
2. Los Angeles (Calif.)—Fiction. 3. Americans—Europe—Fiction.
4. Public prosecutors—Fiction. 5. Self-realization—Fiction.
6. Women travelers—Fiction. 7. Europe—Fiction. I. Title.

PS3607.R495P37 2005
813'.6—dc22
                                                          2005041158

ISBN-13: 978-0-06-078928-2 (pbk.)
ISBN-10: 0-06-078928-X

06 07 08 09 10   BVG/RRD   10 9 8 7 6 5 4 3 2

To all those who are searching for something different
and are willing to travel the world to find it.

Acknowledgments

If it takes a village to raise a child, it takes a community to publish a book. Although I have spent many days writing in solitude, lonely has never called my name, as I've been blessed with family and friends who have always made their presence known. And while there are too many souls who have extended kindness toward me, broken bread with me, fought battles for me, laughed and cried alongside of me, and been loved by me to name off one by one, I'd like to express a special thank-you to the following for their immense contribution to this book:

Mom, the sun that shines on us all.

Dad, Papa, Dwayne, the Texas Gregorys, Richard and Kendra, I love you all with an infinite heart. You are the earth I walk upon.

Thank you, Gina, Kelli, Julia, Janine, Daria, Christine, and Charles, for your enduring friendship. The times you've gone above and beyond the boundaries of friendship have not passed by unnoticed. You are the sky I look up to.

Nia and D'Angela, my newfound treasures, you are the creative rocks I lean on.

Milton and Bess Qualls, my neighbors, my friends, my health gurus. The chick in 6 would have left the building a long time ago without you.

To my attorneys Shawn, Loretha and Tamara, thanks for keeping me out of the big house as well as the poor house.

To my editor at Amistad, Stacey Barney, and my agent,

Manie Barron (and Anna Deroy), thanks for taking a chance on the new broad. May this be the first of many.

Thank you, Karen, for reading every word I've ever written (sometimes twice). Your unwavering support has made this journey a ride worth taking. While I can't promise you "Gayle status," you will always have a sane ear to bend and a bony shoulder to cry on. And a very special thank-you to my sister, Kim. You are the reason I am . . . Tamara Terraine. Mostly, because you named me, but also because you have always nurtured and encouraged me. You are the water that cleanses, sustains, and rejuvenates me. May I never live in a world where you are more than a page away.

Taking Off

One

If you come to a fork in the road, take it.
—*Yogi Berra, American athlete*

I'M TRYING TO BREATHE like I learned in yoga class. It's not working. I only went to yoga once and I hated it. I'm a firm believer that the *try again* adage is bullshit. You've got a fifty-fifty shot of ending up with the same result as you do of having a different one.

"Maya, this is a high-performance automobile. Make it perform, for God's sake."

The 5-series Benz we were rolling in might as well have been a go-cart. I should've left the house earlier. You're supposed to be at the airport two hours before an international flight. I've got an hour and ten minutes before takeoff and Maya is acting like she's the poster child for the Safe Driving Council.

"I can't believe I'm going to miss my flight."

I put my head down on the dashboard and stare at my shoes. Tan Tod loafers. Ideal for traveling, completely wrong for just about anything else. I spot an orange Skittle lying on the black carpet. It's a cruel reminder that not only am I late, but I'm starving, too.

I lift my head just in time to see Maya making a crucial mistake.

"What are you doing? Don't get on the freeway. Take Airport Boulevard!" I'm yelling at her like she's a puppy that's peed on my Jimmy Choos.

She cuts her eyes at me but does as she is told.

"I'm sorry, but you can control more variables if you take surface streets."

"Kia, you need to calm down. You're not going to miss your flight . . ."

She glances at her clock radio. It's 9:00 P.M. on the nose. My flight leaves at 10:05.

Maya continues, "But if you do miss it, it's not because of me. It was your vain behind that spent the last half-hour packing a toiletry bag! How many beauty products does one girl need?"

If we were in a court of law, I would object. I admit to having a healthy amount of self-esteem. I mean, I do think I'm cute. Not Halle cute—more like that black girl who was on three episodes of *Friends* cute.

"I'm a lot of things, Maya, but obnoxiously vain is not one of them."

Maya gives me a motherly pat on the knee. "Oh, honey . . ." she says all sugary-sweet, as only a Georgia peach can. "You haven't stopped looking at yourself in the mirror since we got in the car."

The truth of this statement didn't prevent me from noticing that taking one hand off the wheel has caused her to drive even slower. I try not to freak out about it as I look once more into the visor mirror.

"I'm trying to figure out who is this girl staring back at me."

I'd just had my hair corn-rolled, à la Alicia Keys, and I wasn't sure if I liked it. I also wasn't sure if people could tell. Could they tell that just a few short hours ago my whole world had been rocked? Could they tell that yesterday I was a hotshot lawyer on top of my game and today . . . well, today . . . in between my mani/pedi and my hair appointment, I was summoned to my boss's office and promptly suspended. I'm too embarrassed to talk about it right now. With anyone. It's just one more reason I have to make this flight. The further away I can get from my life the better.

Maya looks me over. "It's certainly a different look for you, but I think it's hot. What did Lorna say?"

Lorna is my mother. She's the quintessential black Stepford wife—perfect, but mouthy. Her hair is always done, dinner is always on the table, and she always has something to say about something.

"I breezed in long enough to grab her travel iron. She took one look at me and said if by some miracle I received an invitation to meet the Queen, I should decline."

Maya guffaws. "Classic."

I laugh along with her. Ouch! My head hurts. These braids are tight as a drum. Any drastic change in my facial expression causes shooting pain across the top of my scalp.

"And for the record, Maya, I was packed two days ago."

I'm one of the few Negroes who take pride in doing things ahead of schedule and openly admit to being a Maroon 5 groupie.

"I swear, Candy's triflin' ass. I sat there for forty-five minutes before she sent Coco over to wash me. If she would've started me on time . . ."

There was no need to finish the thought. Every black woman has beauty-shop horror stories. It's our cross to bear. It's like going to church. We know we have to go, even when we don't feel like it. Afterwards, though, we feel like a different person, like a weight has been lifted off our shoulders. But, good God, why does it have to take so long? Does the pastor really have to take up two collections? Does the hairdresser really have to double-book appointments? Inquiring-minded people with a life really want to know.

For some inexplicable reason Maya comes to a perfectly safe stop on a barely yellow light. A lemony green if you will. I grit my teeth. I'm not trying to get my girl a ticket. I would never encourage anyone to break the law, but the smallest sign of urgency on her part will keep me from clocking her ass if I miss this plane. In an attempt to keep my cool, I continue with my hair saga.

"Then I had to wait even longer because she didn't have the right hair. Can you believe that heifer had the nerve to try and put in some mess she must have cut out of a doll's head? Said it would be fine since I was braiding mine down to the ends."

Fingering her long, jet-black hair, Maya is appropriately appalled. A sure sign of a good friend.

"I told her, if God didn't see fit to plant pubic hair on the top of my head, neither would she."

Maya laughs so hard she actually gives the Mercedes a little gas. Good. All I have to do now is keep the jokes coming.

"I made Coco go and buy some Ethiopian hair from the Korean shop down the street. It's more expensive but at least it won't turn into beady carpet the first time I get it wet in the ocean!"

Maya looks at me curiously. "So, the freeway is off limits, but the ocean qualifies as a controllable entity?"

"They haven't had a shark attack in the Mediterranean in like a hundred years."

Maya laughs. "You read that somewhere?"

"Hey, some people TiVo. Some people salsa. I surf the Net."

"Kia, you really need to get you some."

"Like I don't know that? It's been two months, but it feels like two years."

"You planning on going topless?"

"Isn't that what normally happens when you're getting some?"

"I meant on the beach, Kia."

"I don't know. Maybe. I'll have to see how comfortable I feel since I'm flying solo and all . . ."

She speeds up a bit further. Interesting. Guilt works too. Maya was the first person I asked to come on this trip with me, but like most of those who work behind the scenes in black Hollywood, she's in between gigs. A trip to Europe wouldn't be a prudent move. I offered to cover the hotels—I had to pay for a room anyway—but that still left transportation, sight-seeing costs, and, let's not forget, shopping and food. My girl may be a svelte one hundred and twenty pounds, but the heifer can grub.

Maya now drives behind an elderly man doing twenty in a thirty-five zone. I wait for her to change lanes. She doesn't.

"You know, it's going to be a little hard for me to bring you back a gift from Europe, if I don't actually get to Europe." I'm trying not to sound like a bitch. It's not working.

"Just don't let me look up and find your braided, topless, black butt on the cover of *National Geographic* with a headline reading 'Bush Woman Goes Continental.' "

With friends like these . . .

Maya and I met a few years ago at a Friday girls' night out I'd put together at this swanky bar inside the L'Ermitage hotel in Beverly Hills. Well, it was swanky till the hip-hop crowd discovered it. Now it's just a place where Negroes stand around flashing their bling, holding highball glasses of Courvoisier, yelling, *What up, my nigga* to everyone who passes by. That's the thing about L.A. Places stay trendy for, like, five and a half minutes and then somebody gets shot in a drive-by or overdoses on the curb out front and *poof!* the place might as well be a pair of gauchos!

But the night I met Maya it was all good. The city's black bourgeoisie was out in full force. A group of black male physicians planted themselves in a corner facing the door. Sad to say, not a viable prospect among them. Most were already married or doing their damn best never to be. The thing about doctors is, if you don't snag one before the white coat becomes a permanent part of their wardrobe, you certainly won't snag one afterwards. Unless you're a twenty-two-year-old model (I use the term loosely) and you're willing to sign an extremely constraining prenup.

Across from the docs huddled a small contingent of black-tresses, Gabrielle Union (she's even prettier in person) and the like. They may not have wanted to be seen but certainly were heard with their loud, high-pitched giggles. "Girl, I read for that part, too. Denzel sure takes those test screening kisses seriously . . ."

The eclectic crowd I'd assembled was knocking back apple martinis on the center sofas near the fireplace. All right, they weren't that eclectic. Six bougie, highly educated, and gainfully employed babes, all in various phases of being both over- and underwhelmed by our middle-class lives. Present and accounted for were my sister Diane, a dentist; and Lori, Michelle, and myself, all attorneys. Lori did business affairs for one of the big studios—Universal, to be exact—and had brought along Maya.

Maya is a "D girl." I first thought it applied to her ample breasts, which were very much on display. Not in a tacky Mariah Carey *I just got a boob job and I want everyone to notice* kind of way, but in a relaxed, *Yeah, I got a great set of tits and if you had them you'd show them off too* kind of way. I liked her instantly.

Learning that she wasn't a lawyer or from L.A. like the rest of us made me like her even more. I'm not sure how, but one day I looked up and realized all of my friends were carbon copies of myself. All came from similar backgrounds, black and privileged. All belonged to the same gym, Magic Johnson's 24-

hour Fitness on Slauson (belonging is different from going, as evidenced by my now-pushing-a-size-eight behind). All spent a fair portion of our just-shy-of-six-figure salaries maintaining our pressed or permed tresses. At least Maya had an accent.

I found out later a D girl is a creative type who's responsible for the development of film projects. They do all the work but rarely get any of the credit. The only words of comfort I could offer Maya were, "God gave you beauty and brains. Getting credit for your accomplishments would just be overkill." We've been friends ever since.

Until now. She's back to driving like Miss Daisy.

"What airline are you flying?" Maya asks.

"Uh, American. But you need to go to the International Terminal."

Maya glances at the car clock again. Realizing I have fifty-three minutes left, she swerves right, crossing four lanes of traffic. Speeding through the drop-off lane, she nearly hits a family of five mindlessly crossing the street and comes to a screeching halt right where I need to be. That's my girl!

Maya grunts as she unloads my apparently heavy Tumi cargo bag from her trunk. "What have you got in here?"

"Enough clothes to make me the best-dressed broad abroad . . ." I say while pulling out the matching suitor bag. ". . . And the shoes to match."

Maya plops the aforementioned toiletry bag onto my shoulder. "Let's not forget this."

The wind gets sucked out of me. How can lotion, makeup, and a doo rag weigh so much?

"It's just not right that I'm not going with you," Maya says while giving me a crushing hug.

I smile at her. "You can make up for it by hanging around in case I miss this plane. I'd need a ride home."

She wants to kill me but she knows as well as I do that the

ride or die clause prevails. If you agree to do something for your girl, you've got to do it all the way. All the way in this case means you either hang around to see if I catch my flight, or you drive off with the understanding that your ass will be coming right back if I miss it. Take your pick.

"I'll come back if you need me to," she says in a *you're really working my nerves* sort of way.

"I love you, Maya."

"I love you, too."

Heading for the terminal, I hear Maya call my name. I turn to see her grab a shiny silver-wrapped package accented by a red velvet bow from the backseat of her car. As she tosses it to me I realize that my world is so out of whack at this point that all I can think is, *Great, another fucking thing to carry.*

Maya seems so pleased with herself. "Don't open it until your birthday."

A few weeks ago the thought of spending my thirty-fifth birthday in Paris sounded exciting. Now it just sounds . . . lonely . . . pathetic.

I'm standing on the black rubber thingy that automatically opens doors. People rush past me, but I can't move. My airy light loafers have become concrete boots. We make decisions every day. Most are benign, mundane. I'd say insignificant but only God really knows that. But this is one of those proverbial forks-in-the-road moments. This decision could affect the rest of my life. Or at least the next few weeks of it. If I go inside, nothing but uncertainty awaits me. If I jump back into Maya's car, it'll be the same old same old. Sunday dinners at my parents', Friday-night drinks with the girls, Saturday mornings at the hair salon, Wednesday evenings at singles Bible study, Thursday nights plopped on the couch for NBC Must See TV, blah, blah, blah. All the while stressing out about my suspension. And trying not to stress out about being thirty-five and single. And not a man in sight.

Maya gives me a reassuring smile. "Girl, go on. Europe won't know what hit it. You'll have the time of your life. I promise."

If only Maya had a dick. She always knows what to say and has excellent taste in clothes and restaurants. We'd make a perfect couple.

Not knowing what else to do, I hold tight to my gift. I throw Maya a smile and a wave. And I walk a different road.

Two

People don't take trips—trips take people.
—*John Steinbeck, American author*

THE AIRPORT is where chaos comes to roost.

At Singapore Air, Asian travelers slowly inch forward huge boxes painstakingly wrapped in yards of packaging tape. I'm guessing they're full of gifts for relatives hungry for anything from America, even if the stuff was actually made in Taiwan.

A group of Middle Easterners try to ignore the blatant and hostile stares being hurled their way. I smile sympathetically at a young man wearing a turban who looks to be as comfortable as the only husband at a Mary Kay party. Three years post–9/11 and they're still being treated like social pariahs. But, hey, African-Americans have endured three hundred plus years of it and all we did was take a boat ride.

My cell phone rings.

"Maya, you can't possibly be missing me already?"

"Oh yes I can," I hear a sexy mothafucka say.

Every woman has a G spot. Mine is in my ears. A sweet baritone voice can talk my panties off every time. That being said, though, Barry White, God rest his soul, never had a chance.

Flash is a good-looking brotha currently sporting a perfectly trimmed goatee outlining lips any woman would want to bite into. His strong suit is his flavor, though. He's all about the flavor. I nicknamed him Kool-Aid he has so much flavor. And just like Kool-Aid, he completely lacks in nutritional value.

We dated for about a year. It was cake as long as we were just kicking it. But anytime we tried to make it more than that, one of us would screw it up. He finally had the good sense to put us out of our mutual misery. I was too busy clinging to the false hope that one of us (him) would spontaneously change into the perfect mate the other (me) wanted them to be.

We'd been broken up for nearly a year when I ran into him at a party in Vegas.

Maya and I had scored tickets to the Roy Jones, Jr., fight. After Jones pounded that ass we pounded the Strip in search of a good time. By the third party we were over it. It seemed like half of L.A. had followed us there; we were partying with the same people we'd partied with the week before. And that party sucked.

As we headed out the door, I literally bumped into Flash, and all I could say was, "Damn, you look good!" It's a crying shame when the sexiest man in the room is at the top of your *already been there* list.

Flash looked me up and down, taking an extra beat to appreciate my shoes, knowing that would turn me on. If I'm going to spend good money on the perfect high-heeled open-toe muted gold Prada pumps, the least a man can do is notice them. Flash smiled seductively at me and said, "You, too."

He's been my bootie-call man ever since. Nearly two years now. A once-or-twice-a-month type thing. Nothing too frequent, just enough to keep everything in working order. Can't let a car sit idle for too long without starting the engine unless you want the battery to go dead.

Our last escapade was particularly memorable. Very little

romance. No candles, no R. Kelly, no sexy lingerie. But damn if it wasn't some of the best sex I've ever had. Intense. Rhythmic. Short, short, long.

Two short sweet kisses and one long suck fest. Two short squeezes on the right nipple, one long arousing tug on the left. Two short teasing strokes, one long deep thrust. Short, short, long. Short, short, long.

It went on like this for three hours. Okay, it was nowhere near that long. But who'd want it to be? Too much of a good thing is almost as bad as not enough. Right when I was about to tire of it, he changed up on me. The pace became frenetic, energetic. Our bodies grew sweaty and sticky. It was all about the orgasm now. And, yes, I had three of them.

"Flash, now is really not a good time."

"You're obviously still mad at me about the Vanessa thing."

"Who is Vanessa?"

"The woman I told you about? The one I was kind of feeling?"

My stomach tightens. The American Airlines counter is packed.

"You mentioned you met somebody, Flash. You never told me her name."

"Well, Kia, there's no need to remember it now . . ."

I sense the disappointment in his voice. "Look, I'm really sorry to hear that, but like I said, now is really not a good time. I have to go."

To my amazement, and I'm sure to his, I hang up. I've never done such a thing before, and I must admit, it felt pretty good. This bold move inspires another. Ignoring the hoards of people in front of me, I march to the head of the line.

A Hasidic Jewish man draped in the customary long black coat, wide-brimmed hat, and sideburn curls yells at me. "The line's back here, lady."

"*Obe kobe, Lana Fontana!*" I shout back in a made-up African dialect.

He waves me off in frustration, speaking to no one in particular. "Dumb foreigners make me sick."

Guess you only have to be pious on the Sabbath.

It's amazing what a new hairstyle can do. If I were sporting my usual press and curl, layered and flipped up on the ends, I would've never tried to pass myself off as a straight-up African woman. I guess not looking like yourself can make you not act like yourself. And that's just fine by me. Being me hasn't been so much fun lately.

A bookish airline rep approaches me. I stare at his extremely large glasses and teeny tiny head. How the two found each other I'll never know. But it's clear by the indentations on his nose and the crazy glue holding the left eye and earpiece together, they've been a couple for quite some time. I shove my e-ticket at him. I'm riding this *speak no English* thing for all it's worth.

The rep looks at the ticket and then his watch. Forty-nine minutes to go.

"Nothing like cutting it close, huh, ma'am?"

I freeze up like a black man caught in police headlights. He's trying to be nice, but I'm not supposed to understand him. Luckily, he's more interested in getting me on my flight than in polite conversation.

He calls out to the only open ticketing agent. "Joanne, we got a runner here."

Before rushing to the first-class counter, I enthusiastically shake his hand. Joanne takes my passport without looking at me, as if my lateness has personally offended her.

I try offering an explanation. "You wouldn't believe the day I'm having . . ."

"That's probably because I don't intend to hear about it," she says in a cold British accent. "This will go a lot faster if we by-pass the small talk."

I like the sound of *fast* so I let the dis go. Joanne is obviously under a lot of stress, or PMS-ing at case-study levels.

"I don't suppose there's an aisle seat still open?"

"Sure. On the plane leaving first thing in the morning," she says without looking up from her computer screen.

"Window?" I ask.

No response.

I load my cargo bag onto the scale. Fifty-five pounds. Good. I can do fifteen pounds of shopping without having to pay a penalty.

Joanne finally looks at me. "The possibility of you making this flight is slim. The possibility of your bags making it is none. They'll go out sometime tomorrow."

Joanne does not look like a person who smiles, much less jokes, but I ask anyway.

"You're joking, right?"

"A two-hour check in is customary so that we may do our best to ensure the safety of all travelers. Your late arrival will re-quire us to go through your bag with a fine-tooth comb. You're free to fly with your bags tomorrow. There'll be an additional fee of two hundred dollars, of course."

My American Express card had already taken a serious beat-ing in preparation for this trip. I wasn't shelling out another dime until my feet touched foreign soil.

"Fine. I'll just carry these two on with me."

One too many lost bags flying on Jamaica Air has taught me to pack an extra thong and a blouse in my carry-on. I can sur-vive for a day, maybe two.

"As long as you can run with them. The airplane doors close in eleven minutes," Joanne says handing me my boarding pass.

I throw her a seemingly genuine smile. "My job sucks, too. I'll pray for you."

She seems thrown by my comment, giving me the exact amount of satisfaction I was looking for.

Sprinting to the security checkpoint, my cell rings again.

"I'm going to forget you hung up on me," Flash says in his best *I'm trying to be mature about this* tone. "I want to come with you. I could really use a break from L.A. Some time abroad would be good for me creatively."

Flash is a freelance photographer. I was initially turned off by the name/occupation connection. But since his given name is Frederick Leonard Sherman, I let it slide. If Dallas Raines can do weather, I guess Flash can take pictures.

"I'm at the airport as we speak, can you be here in say . . . now?"

"No, smart-ass, but I could meet you in a week or so. Where will you be then?"

"Paris."

"Bet. I never get tired of doing the Louvre," Flash says excitedly.

For a moment I picture us exploring the City of Light, strolling hand in hand down the Champs-Élysées, sipping fine champagne not from a flute but off each other's lips. That could be a cute vacation. Except I know that after three days of coochie-blowing sex, he'll start to get on my nerves. He's moved by art. I'm moved by information. He thinks he's a creative genius. I think he takes cool pictures of models. He thinks I'm a patsy for the Man because I work in the DA's office. He's probably right, but screw him for not being more supportive. Flash coming with me to Europe will just be more of the same, with an upgrade in location. No. Thank. You.

Then there's Vanessa. Flash's photography has allowed him

to travel the world over. He goes to Paris about as often as I go to New York. Once a year or so. It's why I foolishly asked him to come along. That's when he told me about her. He said he'd met this great woman about a month before (which would explain why I haven't really heard from him) and although it was too early to proclaim them an exclusive couple, he didn't think she'd take to the idea of him traipsing through Europe with his ex. While I respected his attempt at being a stand-up guy, it pissed me off that it was coming at my expense. And now what? I'm supposed to forget I'm just a seat filler till the next Vanessa comes along? I know bootie calls have a shelf life, but I was hoping his use-by date would expire before mine. That I'd be the one who'd put an end to our sexcapades, not him.

"Flash, I was wrong to violate the bootie-call credo: Thou shalt forgo all vertical activity, unless you're naked. Thou shalt not spend more than three consecutive days together, unless you're naked . . ."

I'm prepared to recite all ten but he cuts me off. "Kia, you know I've never been one for rules."

"Yeah, well, I'm a stickler about them, so I'm going to have to pass on your Johnny-come-way-too-lately offer. Thanks for the great orgasms and everything, but I think we've taken this bootie-call thing as far it can go. Forgive the cliché, but I hope we can still be friends. When I get back, we should hook up and I'll show you my vacation photos. Over lunch."

I hang up. And this time I turn the damn phone off.

Three

There are only two emotions in a plane: boredom and terror.

　　　　　　　　—*Orson Welles, American actor*

F11. I'M LOOKING FOR F11. *Lord, please let the gate numbers go in descending order*. It's probably a futile prayer but I serve a big God, anything is possible.

Sure enough, as I turn the corner, a huge sign reading "F1" greets me. I begin my long pilgrimage to Mecca, otherwise known as the last gate on the tarmac. I count off the gates as I fly by.

"F2. F3 . . ." I ignore the pain pulsating through my right shoulder as I run with my bags. "F5. F6 . . ."

I'm sweating. What happens to cashmere when it gets wet, I wonder. If this baby-blue, Juicy Couture, three-hundred-dollar sweat suit shrinks up on me, I'll die.

"F9 . . ." I hit hyper-speed as I see the F11 gate agents shutting down the check-in counter.

"Wait," I scream. "I'm supposed to be on that plane!"

"We called final boarding ten minutes ago," a femme male agent says with a raised eyebrow.

I raise an eyebrow back at him. "I know my tardiness is an affront to God, country, and the Queen, but I prefer to make my apologies in person, and that hinges upon me making this flight."

"We don't have time for this, Peter. Let her on," a British woman shouts from inside the doorway of the 767.

Finally, someone who understands I'm not an enemy of the aviation industry. I don't have a bomb hidden in my shoe, or a box cutter in my purse.

Being careful not to rumple her crisp uniform, I throw my arms around the bony brunette who just made my day. "Thank you, thank you, thank you." The embrace is brief, as some of the other flight attendants stare at me disapprovingly. "I didn't just violate some FAA regulation, did I?"

"Several, actually. But I prefer spontaneous gestures over staid decorum any day," she says, sliding her meticulously tied scarf a quarter-inch to the left. Her neck is about the size of a grown man's wrist.

The ease with which she smiles at me suggests it's something she likes to do often. I try to smile back, but my scalp really hurts. I gingerly rub my sore temples.

Karin (that's how it's spelled on her name tag) begins locking the plane's giant doors.

"You'll need to hurry to your seat. Joanne called from the ticketing counter and told us to keep a look out. We've been waiting for you."

I feel bad. I wasn't really going to pray for her. It was just one of my many courtroom tactics; show up the bad guy without looking like one yourself.

Making my way to 52E, it becomes uncomfortably clear that this plane is packed to the rafters.

"Oops, sorry, sir," I say nicely as my bag bangs into the knee of 45G.

I'm too embarrassed to look back, but by the sounds of it I hit a nerve.

Forty-eight, forty-nine . . . oh God, please don't let that be my seat!

Fifty-two C and D are currently occupied by an obviously sleep-deprived mother and her wailing six-month-old baby. And squeezed into 52F is, without a doubt, the largest man I've ever seen. I try not to let my disappointment show. A hundred pairs of sympathetic eyes fall upon me. I don't need your sympathy, people! I need an escape hatch.

I call upon every Christian bone in my body, trying not to act ugly. Motherhood and an overactive thyroid are not crimes. I eke out what I hope resembles a kind smile. Relieved I'm not making a scene, 52F smiles back. He seems like a sweet guy. Maybe the baby won't cry for the entire flight. Resigning myself to the situation, I begin the arduous search for a place to put my bags. A full flight means full overhead bins. I'm sweating again. Fifty-eight . . . nope . . . 61, 62 . . . no, no. Defeated, I head back the other way.

As I drag my homeless bags forward, a voice comes over the PA system.

"Ladies and gentlemen, we cannot take off until everyone is in their seat with their seatbelt fastened."

"I'm doing the best I can here, lady!" I mumble under my breath.

Maybe this is a sign? What if God is trying to warn me the pilot is operating on too few hours' sleep and this baby is going down over the Atlantic Ocean? What if Osama is ordering an attack on Buckingham Palace the day I'm planning to visit? I shouldn't be taking a vacation right now, anyway. I should be home combing through the classifieds, trying to find a new job, or at the very least coming up with a strategy to keep my current one.

The weight of the entire day hits me as I take another look at Bob's Big Boy and Cry Baby Sue, and damn if I don't start crying, too. What am I doing? I don't cry in public, and quite frankly, I hate people who do. Crying is strictly a private affair, preferably done at home. Behind closed doors. With the shades drawn.

Again the flight crew looks glaringly in my direction. I pray they decide I'm not stable enough to fly and kick me off this sucker. Karin is elected to come deal with me.

"What seems to be the problem, miss?"

"I don't think I want to go. What if I hate the food? What if I don't understand what people are saying?" I sound like I'm trying to avoid the first day of kindergarten.

"It's London. I guarantee you'll hate the food. Last I checked, though, aside from a few idioms here and there, you shouldn't have a problem understanding us."

A Brit with a sense of humor; I like that. But it doesn't stop the tears.

"I heard the French are rude and the Greeks are crazy. I can get all of that at a family reunion."

Karin laughs but doesn't seem to have a comeback for that one.

"This just isn't my day. I can't feel my right arm. My braids are giving me a migraine. I got suspended from my job. I just broke up with a guy who isn't even my boyfriend. And now, I don't have anywhere to put my bags!"

"I'll store them up front. Now, where is your seat? We really need to get this plane off the ground."

I point in the general direction of where my seat should be. My friend in 52F has had to raise the armrest separating our seats in order to actually fit into his. Meanwhile, the baby has thrown her bottle, teething ring, and saliva-soaked plush toy onto what is the remaining open area.

"Oh, my," Karin murmurs.

She grabs my bag and pulls me toward the front of the plane. Yes! I'm getting off this flying trapeze. As we rush past row after row, it suddenly occurs to me that maybe I'm not going home. My behavior has been a little suspect and could be seen as interfering with the flight. A clear FAA infraction. Maybe I'm going to jail.

"Karin, I'm being a baby about this. My seat is fine."

As she continues to pull me forward—32, 31, 30—I tell myself I'm overreacting. I might be detained and have to pay a huge fine, but I won't go to jail. This brings me little comfort as I see the exit sign ahead on the right. As we enter the first-class cabin, I plead with Karin one last time.

"Just let me go back to my seat and I swear you won't hear a peep out of me again. You don't even have to bring me peanuts."

"Relax. This is your seat. Now just sit down. Shut up. And let us take off. I'll come back to check on you once the seatbelt signs are off."

Karin shoves my bags into a roomy overhead bin and plops herself into a rear-facing fold-down seat.

As soon as my butt hits the spacious, comfy aisle seat of 4E, I'm instantly transported into one of those classic movie moments. The one where it's pouring down rain and just as the star-crossed lovers finally kiss, the clouds give way to sunny blue skies. My tears dry on the spot and I suddenly feel as though everything is going to be okay. Yep, this trip is exactly what I needed. That and a drink. Hel-*lo*? Can we get this baby up in the air? Momma needs a glass of the bubbly.

I settle further into my seat and smile. Maya was right. I'm going to have the time of my life.

Pre-Boarding

Four

The world is a book, and those who do not travel read only one page.

—*Saint Augustine, African clergyman*

SIX WEEKS. What the hell am I supposed to do with myself for six weeks? There's only so much shopping, soul searching, catching up on doctor's appointments, or reconnecting with old friends a girl can do.

Six weeks. That's like maternity leave. It's long enough to get a life-altering boob job, tummy tuck, chin implant, and a celebrity-white smile on *Extreme Makeover*.

It's a frickin' long time. And I don't do idle very well. Never have. Six weeks off with nothing to do could kill me.

Growing up, summer vacations were sheer torture. To my mother's chagrin, I stopped napping at the age of three. From then on, every second had to be filled with activity: Girl Scouts, ballet, piano, and, finally (some time around middle school), sewing classes. Since I loved clothes, and a sewing machine was cheaper than a piano, it was a match made in Heaven for all concerned.

I put my head down on my desk and stare at my shoes. Black-croc, round-toe Gucci pumps. I'm slipping on my grooming detail. My left ankle is a bit on the ashy side.

"This city needs to get its act together and pay people in dollars instead of time off," Guy Torres, a Hispanic wannabe white boy said as he walked into the office. "I had plans for that money. I was all set to buy the new Z4 BMW roadster. I'll bust a nut if Drew pulls up in one before I do."

Can't bust what you don't have, I think to myself. Guillermo was his real name but he thought Guy would open more doors. Not that his pandering has translated into him being treated any better than the rest of us token minorities in the DA's office. But it doesn't stop him from giving it the college-frat-boy try.

There are two kinds of minorities who work here. Sellouts like Guy and suckas like me. Guy believes the system works; the reason there are so many minorities in prison is because they're the ones committing all the crimes. I believe the system is detrimentally flawed; the reason there are so many minorities in prison is because that's the way the powers that be want it. I fight on a daily basis to tip the scales of justice in our favor, and while I may win a battle here and there, I'm clearly losing the war.

"Drew isn't showing up in a Z4," I declared.

"How do you know? Did he tell you what he's getting?"

"I didn't have to," Drew said, breezing into the room. "She knows I wouldn't be caught dead in a punk car."

Resources being what they are in city government, office space is hard to come by. Only the bigwigs get their own office, forcing those of us on the come-up to share. Initially I thought Guy and I would forge a colored-people coalition, but it turned out that Drew and I actually had more in common. We're both prochoice, anti–death penalty default Democrats who appreciate the finer things in life but wouldn't sell our souls to the devil to obtain or to keep them. Guy, being our polar opposite, quickly became the annoying little brother who always tagged along because Mom said he had to.

For three years, we've been overhearing each other's telephone conversations, reading each other's mail, eating each other's meals—inevitably bonding, all on the tax payer's dollar, through life's highs and lows—birthdays, breakups, family funerals, promotions.

Drew was promoted first, after getting assigned to a police-corruption case. The televized trial made Drew an instant media darling. At six foot three, with brownish-gold eyes and a head full of dark curly hair that he wore rather long in order to cover his big ears, he was what one might call *easy on the eyes*. A lot of the girls in the office had a crush on him. Quite a few of the guys, too. As white boys go, he was all right. Mostly because he didn't try too hard. He was charming but not a flirt. Smart without being a know-it-all. Of course, I'd just as soon grow my perm out and run around town nappy-headed before I'd say any of this to his face. His ego gets pumped up enough around here. From the DA on down to the security staff.

"I brought us a pity pizza," Drew said, sliding the box over to me.

Inside was a thin-crust margarita pizza with olives. Just the way I like it. Taking a huge unladylike bite, I stewed over the injustice of the situation. Time off in lieu of overtime pay hardly seemed fair in light of my recent winning performances. Thanks to me, the Christian Academy High School cheerleader who poisoned her football-playing boyfriend's Gatorade because he slept with the drill team captain is serving ten years. The dentist who whacked his wife so he could marry a crooked Blue Cross claims secretary is doing life plus. We didn't even have a body for the first three weeks of the trial, but her torso was eventually found inside a refrigerator at a popular dumping ground. My boss, District Attorney Holden, was thrilled to the point of boyish glee. Getting the dentist on insurance fraud alone wasn't going to grab the media attention he so unabashedly seeks.

But she quickly turned to pissy when in a quote in the *L.A. Times* I mistakenly thanked a witness who had the courage to testify in a tough case but failed to pay homage to the almighty DA.

"Ms. Carson, are you aware this is an election year?"

"Yes, sir, the first Tuesday in November."

"Glad to see you paid attention in civics class. It's just PR 101 you flunked. Never waste an opportunity to thank the hand that feeds you."

I thought I'd done that. Everyone knows the case came down to one thing: the witness I delivered. Belinda Maxwell had no intention of testifying against her boyfriend, Myron "Junior" Simmons, a big-time drug dealer up on a murder charge.

Belinda was a true-blue, acrylic-nail-wearing ghetto princess. Hundreds of micro braids that should have been taken out weeks ago surrounded her attractive face. Had life been any easier or more kind, she'd be considered pretty. There was a hardness about her face that only a life filled with worry and heartbreak can bring.

The police wanted Belinda's man bad. He'd been arrested twelve times but nothing serious ever stuck beyond a two-year stint he did in Mohave on a probation violation. It was there that Junior was able to make a rep for himself.

While the warden couldn't prove it, word on the street had it that Junior shanked his street rival to death in the shower. The day he was released from prison his empire doubled, giving him control of a five-square-mile section of Compton. Death and mayhem quickly became the order of the day. All the cops and the community could do was run for cover.

Holden assigned me second chair to Guy's lead council, meaning it was his call on how to approach Belinda about testifying for the prosecution. As we traveled deep into the hood and knocked on her door, I tried to advise him on how to handle her, but he wasn't having it. He played the *it's your duty as an American citizen, as a member of a civilized society* card. One look into Belinda's eyes told me she knew better than most how uncivilized society could be.

Belinda and I both knew it wasn't her citizenship that fucked her till she almost understood the meaning of life. Nor was it the grand ol' flag that made her feel safe on the nights when gunshots went off like microwave popcorn. It didn't take a cum laude grad to surmise that Junior had probably done more for Belinda than anybody ever had and she wasn't going to rat him out.

Lacking the desire to see the world beyond his very skewed vision, Guy next played the *you must be in on it* card.

"Belinda, it was your Escalade that was seen fleeing the murder scene. Maybe you drove as Junior fired shots out of the passenger window? I can have you brought in for questioning. Cart off everything you own if we suspect it's been bought with drug money. In short, I can make your life a living hell," Guy told her.

Belinda laughed so hard she snorted Mountain Dew out of her nose.

"I quit high school because I got pregnant by my mom's boyfriend. The only job I've ever been able to hold on to I was just fired from because I got no way to get there since you impounded my ride. I was born a bitch, black, and broke. You can't kick me no lower."

As she reached across her black-lacquer dining table for a Newport, I caught sight of the tattoo plastered generously across her left bicep, a blood-red heart with a bullet ripping a hole through the center of it.

"If you think I'm gonna help send the only decent dick I've ever had to jail, you're smoking more crack than Junior ever thought about selling. There ain't jack you can do to me that hasn't been done already. Junior was here with the kids and me all night. And I'll swear to it in court. After all, it's my duty as an American an' shit."

I fought back a smile. The girl's got game. And plenty of it.

"Put a call in to Big Momma, then. Your kids are gonna need a baby-sitter when we haul you down to County. In hand-cuffs. Come on, Kia. We're done here."

Guy tried to make a dramatic TV exit but I ruined it for him.

"I'll meet you outside in a minute."

The look he shot me said he wasn't happy about having to wait in the car on this side of town, but that's what he gets for not listening to me.

I reached for Belinda's smokes. "Do you mind?"

She looked surprised. She didn't think an uppity bitch like me (girls from this part of town always think girls like me are uppity) would smoke Newports. And she certainly didn't expect an uppity bitch like me to ask before taking something that belonged to her. Nobody else did.

"Every time I try to quit, something happens, you know? Somebody dies, a boyfriend breaks up with me . . ."

I was betting Belinda knew all about those kinds of setbacks. She nods it's okay for me to have a cigarette.

"Belinda, you're risking an awful lot for some decent action. I could see it if it was Super Dick we were talking about . . ."

As I reached for the lighter, I prayed I wouldn't cough. I'd lose her for sure if I did. As far as Belinda was concerned, the only thing we had in common was her cigarettes. Her nasty, disgusting, menthol cigarettes. I smoked it like a pro.

"It's not the dick I'll miss, it's the benjamins that come with it," Belinda replied.

My mother had a similar saying. Funny how that works. Lil' Kim and Condaleeza Rice have more in common than Belinda

Maxwell and Lorna Carson. Yet, you bring a man into it, and we're 3.5 billion peas in a pod.

"I can understand that. What I don't understand is why he had to use your car. He's been through the system enough to know we'd impound it. Strip it down looking for evidence."

I could tell she wasn't thrilled with the idea of cops tearing up the nicest thing she's ever owned.

"It's probably why you haven't visited him yet in jail. No way to get there."

Belinda slurped her soda. I was starting to piss her off.

"Luckily his crew's been coming through. And his momma and his sister . . ."

"Junior doesn't have no sisters," Belinda answered tightly.

"Really? Huh."

I pretended to search through my briefcase for a piece of paper I knew was right on top. It's a copy of the inmate visitor sign-in sheet. I slid it in between the two of us. In order to read it, she'd have to reach for it.

"I just assumed with so many visits she had to be family," I added.

Belinda took in a long puff. I began sliding the sheet back toward my side of the table. She stopped me. Her limited amount of education did not prevent her from seeing that the name Shalita Moore appeared on the sheet eight times. As did the name Myron Simmons III.

"That son of a bitch!" Belinda said, throwing her soda can across the room. "He told me he'd never hit that shit cuz she got too fat. He never said he was the reason for it."

I stubbed out my cigarette. My work was done. She might not testify out of civic duty, but she would out of spite.

I don't like to think of myself as a woman who runs around telling other women what their men are up to. A woman knows when her man is cheating on her. If she doesn't, it's because she doesn't want to know.

I don't begrudge a woman's right to live in the land of denial. You want to believe Prince Charming is coming to rescue your thirty-nine-year-old still-single behind? Be my guest. You think your ever-swelling thighs can still fit into the jeans you bought two years ago? Go right ahead. You want to think that your drug-dealing murderous boyfriend loves you and only you? Fine, as long as it doesn't interfere with my case. Because quiet as it's kept, I've got a little game, too.

Two weeks later we called Belinda in as a hostile witness. She was eager to testify; she just didn't want it to look that way. Junior is now serving twenty years upstate. Shalita and little Myron Simmons III have yet to visit.

Five

If an ass goes traveling, he'll not come home a
horse.

—*Thomas Fuller, English clergyman*

"I'M FLYING, who's buying?"

Two hours after polishing off Drew's pizza, the carbohydrate malaise had set in and I needed a jolt.

Guy threw me five bucks. "A Starbucks run. Great. Get me a tall iced soy caffè mocha with syrup."

"Where have you been, Guy? Carson doesn't do Starbucks. Too robust for her sensitive palate. She prefers her coffee mild, like her men," Drew explained.

"Per your usual, you only got half the story right. Now, am I getting you coffee or not?" I asked.

Drew studied me for a beat.

"What?" I said testily.

"I'm trying to figure out why you're still single? You're so pleasant to be around."

I snatched the ten bucks Drew held out for me.

"You know what you need?"

I shot Drew a death glare.

"Get your mind out of the gutter, Carson. I was just going to say that you need a vacation. We all do. Maybe we're looking at this forced time-off thing all wrong. With the time we've got coming to us we can go anywhere in the world. Backpacking in the Amazon. A safari in Africa. Carson, you could spa your way across Europe. Maybe even party your way through the Greek Isles. You'll be a big hit over there."

"And why is that?"

"You know we Greek men love big booties," Drew replied.

"You don't need to be looking back there. And if I remember correctly, your ex-girlfriend was all T and no A."

Drew smirks at me. "Why do you think she's my ex-girlfriend."

"You know Latin men love big booties, too."

I ignored Guy's futile attempt to join in the fun. A twinge of excitement ran through me as I thought about Europe. Maya and I had talked about going for New Year's 2002. But then 9/11 happened and we ended up going to Puffy's party in Miami instead. It was cute for a minute. But let's face it, brothas ain't checking for a girl like me when hoochies are dropping it like it's hot everywhere.

Not that I build my vacations around finding a man, but it's always been a fantasy of mine to meet one on an airplane. There's something about meeting the man of my dreams at thirty thousand feet that just sounds sexy. It sure beats saying, *We met on the Internet*.

"Carson, I could use the walk. I'll go with you," Drew said, interrupting my mile-high fantasy.

"Suit yourself. But you're still buying," I said waving the ten dollars he just handed me under his nose.

The Coffee Bean and Tea Leaf was a two-block jaunt from the office. Walking down the street, Drew and I must've made quite a sight. Both of us sporting two-hundred-dollar sunglasses, designer pinstriped suits—bought off the rack but fitting like couture—and the ever-present attorney's arrogant grin.

"So, Drew, how's the break-up going?"

"You know how it is. Last week Cassie never wanted to talk to me again. This week she's called three times, begging me to come over."

"Don't do it."

"Why? Are you the only woman in town mature enough to sleep with her ex and expect nothing in return?"

I feigned offense. "You make it sound so tawdry."

"Hey, Carson, it's cool if that's all you're looking for . . ."

"Drew, it's not like guys are beating down my door . . ."

"What about Harrison from the PD's office? He asked you out, didn't he?"

"He has tits! I may have to one day acquiesce and date a pot-belly, but tits are out of the question."

"You have no idea what you're missing out on. Personally, I look forward to the day when I have two sets of ta-tas in bed with me."

"And I look forward to one day meeting the man who doesn't have the same fantasy."

Drew laughed me off. "What about Ken Johnson? What was wrong with him?"

"Come on, Drew, he's a Republican. He makes Guy look like Cesar Chavez."

"I'm just trying to figure it out is all . . ."

I was afraid to ask. But I did anyway. "Figure what out?"

"Are you still making time with Clash because there really is no one else out there for you or because you don't *want* there to be?"

"Why you feel the need to desecrate the man's name, I'll never know."

"Because it irks you so. Feel free to answer my question anytime you like," he said, trying to keep the conversation on track.

I wanted to say, *Feel free to F off*, but I didn't.

"I don't have to defend my relationship with Flash to you, okay? You just need to stay out of grown folks' business."

I don't often call up old black grandmomma sayings when I'm in mixed company, but I knew it would put an end to his line of questioning. He'd hit a nerve and I didn't like it. The public spin has always been that Flash is still in my life simply because I still enjoy having sex with him. But on the DL, it has occurred to me that I might, once again, be keeping Flash around under the misguided hope that he'd change. How pathetic is that? It had also occurred to me that by keeping him around I might be blocking my blessing. God isn't going to send me Mr. Right as long as I'm still fooling around with Mr. Wrong. But what if Flash is really just Mr. Wrong For Now? Maybe that's why I haven't found myself attracted to anyone else, no matter how hard I look? Geez, I should've gone for coffee by myself. I needed caffeine, not a relationship rescue session with Dr. Phil.

I made sure the conversation stayed only on work for the walk back. I mean, Drew and I were cool, we often needled each other about this or that, but the teasing always stayed on the surface. Today he somehow managed to cross a line I didn't even know existed.

"How's the Juarez case going?" I asked.

"He's toast."

Salvador Juarez was a big-time drug dealer who had moved into illegal immigrant smuggling. While the male passengers were required to pay their passage up front, Juarez would usher women across the border for free. Of course when they arrived in the U.S., the women were forced to work off their passage by becoming sex slaves.

"Did you hear how the police finally nabbed him?"

I shook my head and slurped on my blended mocha with whip.

"Some john insisted that the girl he paid a whopping twenty dollars for, call him *Papi*. She kept calling him *Tio* instead. It wasn't until he slapped her around a few times that he realized he was about to bonk his twelve-year-old niece."

"Get out!"

"He was going to keep quiet about the whole thing, but Juarez refused to let the girl go until she worked off her debt."

"I'll trade your twelve-year-old victim for my two fourteen-year-old perpetrators."

Drew shook his head. "I hate trying kids. It makes me feel like a bully on the playground."

"Tell me about it. It's cases like this that make me want to go into retail."

"Why don't you switch sides and go work for the Public Defender's office, Carson?"

"Helping a guilty kid walk out of jail is no less troubling than putting an innocent one in."

"Well, if you go into retail you won't be able to afford five-dollar coffees."

"Hey, where's Guy's coffee?" I asked, already knowing the answer.

"*You* took his money, not me."

This is not the first time that Drew and I have gone out and forgotten to bring Guy back his order. Never on purpose, it just always looks that way.

"Do you remember what he wanted?" I asked.

Drew laughed. "I don't listen when he talks any more than you do."

Screwing up Guy's order wasn't virgin territory for us, either. Unaware of his ever-increasing food allergies, we'd almost killed the poor SOB twice. Once by substituting two-percent milk for soy. Completely lactose intolerant, he spent the remainder of that afternoon glued to a toilet seat. The second time we remembered the soy but went with a vanilla almond syrup, unaware he was severely allergic to nuts. Two sips later we had to rush him to the ER.

As Drew and I headed back to the Coffee Bean, one thought struck me, and struck me hard—I really did need a vacation.

Six

> How much a dunce that has been sent to roam
> excels a dunce that has been kept at home.
> —*William Cowper, English poet*

DECIDING TO GO TO EUROPE was easy. Drew's travel agent, Barb, at American Express, convinced me in one phone call that she could pull together an unforgettable yet affordable excursion. Finding someone to tag along was more of a challenge. I was on my way to Sunday dinner with my family praying that somewhere between the mixed greens with pecans salad and the peach cobbler I could convince my sister, Diane, to accompany me.

It's a short drive from my condo in Culver City to my parents' house in Ladera Heights. It's a small city just shy of three miles wide, located six miles east of the beach and three miles west of the hood. Most of the residents are African-American, married, college-educated, and pulling in around ninety G's annually. Forty years ago white folks abandoned the place when people like my parents started moving in. Now they're clamoring to move back, as property values have skyrocketed, making Ladera one of the most coveted neighborhoods in L.A.

After pulling into my parents' driveway, I jumped out of the car, hoping the neighbor was too engrossed in her gardening to notice me. Mrs. Manning is a member of a group my mother jokingly refers to as "The Apostles." Despite being five Jesus-followers short, these women have deemed themselves responsible for setting the moral tone for the community. Despite being six witches short, I secretly dubbed them "The Coven."

"Hey there, Kia!"

Shoot! I've been spotted. "How are you, Mrs. Manning?"

"I'm still able to go, even though my arthritis keeps acting up. Is that a new car?"

"No, ma'am."

She knows it's not new, she's just setting me up for the okey doke.

She sends me a genteel smile. "You keep it looking so clean. It's a wonder you can't find a man who'd want to ride in it with you."

She and my mother were obviously in cahoots. The neighborhood watch has an ordinance against single women. We're a threat to all that is good and decent.

This was made clear to me more times than I care to remember at my parents' socials. Mom insisted they be called that because "parties" required a big to-do. Invitations had to be sent, a theme had to be chosen. Socials were casual *swing by if you're in the neighborhood* type affairs. Parties without the preamble or the pressure.

To attend one of Lorna Carson's socials was to know what it is to live in class-conscious India. The hierarchy went like this: babies' mommas were the untouchables. They were single and trampy. Harlots to be avoided at all costs. Single women belonged to the polluted laborers' class and simply couldn't be trusted. Something was obviously wrong with them. Especially the ones who went around claiming they didn't need a man to make them happy. My mother always sucked her teeth on that one before saying to whatever uninvited creature made this claim. "It's not the man that makes you happy . . . It's the security from his paychecks. The man's just there to keep you company. And as much as I enjoy having company, sooner or later they'll wear out their welcome."

My mother would then hold her gaze on the woman for a beat and then turn, nice as pie, to any married woman in the room, usually Mrs. Manning and say, "Dotty, have you tried the artichoke dip?"

The two of them would scurry off to the kitchen to blast the woman to kingdom come and back. Minutes later, when the single woman tried to make a quiet exit, my mother would feign surprise.

"Leaving so soon? But the party is just getting started." All said, of course, as she's ushering the woman out the front door.

Next came married women without kids, who essentially made up the bottom rung of the ruling class. The lack of snotty-nosed brats is a clear indication the marriage is in trouble. Need to keep an eye on them.

Second place goes to the newlywed, a crowd favorite unless the bride brags too much about how happy she is. That's a no-no, too, around these here parts.

The winner and still reigning champion is the married woman with kids. They are the Chosen People. Clearly God loves them best because he has given them the most. Never mind that they may be miserable or can barely stand the sight of the man they are tied to till eternity. They rule Ladera Heights, and if you don't like it, move out. Good luck, though, finding a decent, safe neighborhood that doesn't share a similar philosophy.

Before darting into the house, I threw Mrs. Manning a jab of my own.

"Sorry to hear about Julie's troubles. If they ever make adultery a crime, I'll drag that cheating son-in-law of yours into court so fast . . ."

"Ouch," Mrs. Manning said as she pricked herself on her rosebush.

I smiled triumphantly before heading inside.

Seven

The journey of a thousand miles begins with one step.

—*Lao-tzu, Chinese philosopher*

"WHERE'S LEO?" I asked my sister, stepping into the family room.

"He's sick. I'm bringing him home a plate later."

Twisted as it was, I saw that as a good sign. I felt bad Leo felt bad, but this would be easier without him nosing around. I dumped a bunch of travel brochures into Diane's lap.

"What's all this?" Diane asked.

She'd made herself quite comfortable on the family room couch. I squeezed in next to her.

"Europe. Twenty countries to choose from. I've ruled out Russia, Estonia, Turkey, Poland . . ."

"What killed it for them? Food? Fashion? Fuck options?"

"Fuck options?" I asked.

"That cutie Diane Lane had the affair with in *Unfaithful*—yes. Pope John Paul? No. One's French, the other's Polish."

My baby sister is a hoot. You never know what is going to come out of her mouth, and she swears she filters.

She and her husband share a thriving dental practice in Inglewood. In the three years they've been married, they've purchased the appropriate home in La Fayette Square, another black bougie enclave white folks are dying to reclaim. They own the appropriate numbers of cars, three for every two drivers in the home. They have yet, however, to have the appropriate number of children. If there is any justice in the world, I will at least have met my future husband before she drops her firstborn.

"Oh, Amsterdam . . ." Diane said excitedly as she thumbed through a booklet.

"Should've known a crack head like you would want to go there."

"To quote Mrs. Bobby Brown, 'crack is wack.' I've done my fair share of marijuana, a little coke, ecstasy, shrooms. Once. And if a patient works my nerves, I might take a tiny hit of laughing gas. Just to take the edge off at the end of the day. But never, ever have these lips touched anybody's crack. Pipe."

I busted out laughing. "You are so nasty. Does your momma know you're a stone cold freak?"

"I come by it honestly."

"Di, our mother still calls her vagina her *private place*."

"Please believe Daddy would've left her nosy Rosy behind if her private place wasn't constantly open for business."

The thought of my mother having great sex unnerved me. It would mean she was human, ruining the fantasy I've created that she's really a robot, which explains the weekly repetitive question-and-answer session she puts me through: Why haven't you met anyone? When are you going to settle down and give me some grandchildren? Why aren't you wearing a slip under that dress?

I'm able to endure the Chinese water torture because I know she can't help herself. She was programmed to ask me the same questions over and over and over again. The ability to then turn around and be able to have buck wild sex just doesn't seem fair.

"At the very least she swallows," Diane continued.

"Shut up. You're freaking me out."

"You know both Aunt CeCe and Aunt Vera died of breast cancer. And both were total prudes."

"What's up with your fascination with old people and their sexual appetites?"

"A study just came out saying women who swallow were less likely to get breast cancer. Mom's the oldest and she's walking around cancer free. Dad's sperm must be some powerful stuff," Diane said.

I laughed. "You were obviously dropped on your head as a child. It's not too late for us to sue."

Diane continued sorting through the brochures. "Kia, you know Leo is not going to go for this."

"Didn't he go on a week-long golf tour with his frat brothers last year? Why can't you take a trip with your real sister for her birthday?"

Diane tilted her head at me, indicating I'd made a good point. "What are we talking here? A week in August?"

"We're talking three weeks or the whole month of August. If we're going to trek all the way over there we might as well stay a while," I said.

"Kia, I can't take a month off. I don't get vacation pay."

An obvious statement. One I had somehow overlooked. "Well, how much time can you take off?"

"Ten days, tops," Diane answered.

"I guess we could shuttle through Europe in ten days."

"Or we could go to Jamaica. Lie on the beach in Negril and chill." Her tone suggested this would be her dream vacation.

"I've done the Caribbean thing to death. I'm going to come back with nothing more than a suntan, mosquito bites, and tales of a brief fling with a parasailing instructor."

"And the problem with that is . . ." Diane asked.

"Don't you get tired of doing the same thing, the same way, with the same people?"

"I'm married. Of course I get tired of doing the same thing, the same way, with the same mothafucka. What's your point?"

"This just isn't how I saw my life going down."

"God, Kia, you're gonna meet a man soon," Diane said, shooting a verbal spitball at me.

"I'm not even talking about that!"

Her look said she wasn't buying it.

"All right, I'm not talking just about that."

No point in having the conversation if I wasn't going to be honest.

"Oh, Di, I foolishly thought somehow my law degree entitled me to a lifetime of interesting conversation with fascinating people. At the very least, I thought my work would fulfill me."

"Hey, I look into people's smelly, dirty mouths for a living."

"I'm bored out of my mind, Di. Aside from learning our mother is a freak, I can't remember the last time something caught me by surprise."

"And what? Europe is the surprise capital of the world?"

The chances of her agreeing to go with me were slim if I punched her. So I held back.

"You never wanted to travel abroad?"

"Leo and I went to Italy for our honeymoon, remember? We had a ball," Diane said.

"All the more reason you should come with me. I can't go by myself."

Diane looks at the brochure and then back at me. "August is when the Europeans take their vacations. It could be fun. Maybe I could stretch it to two weeks."

I pounced on my sister, giving her a big hug. "Thank you, thank you, thank you!"

"Don't thank me yet. My husband has to sign off on this."

"Leo is putty in your hands. We're as good as gone."

"Since I can't go for the whole month, maybe Flash could

meet you over there for the second two weeks?" Diane had a sinister smile on her face. "Nothing in the rulebook says bootie calls can't go international. Maybe spending time together over there will help you guys see you should be spending more time together over here?"

"Di, you don't even like the guy, why would you want me to be with him?"

"It's not that I don't like him, I just don't *get* him. You're frickin' prime real estate. Why isn't he closing the deal? What else could he possibly be in the market for?"

"When did I give you the impression that the only thing standing between Flash and me is that he wouldn't close the deal? The truth is, we get along a lot better in bed than we ever did out of it. It's not like we're soul mates or anything."

"When I find the person who planted it into our brains that the man we marry has to be our frickin' soul mate, you're going to need to post my bail, because I'm going to jack her up."

I chuckled loudly.

"I'm serious, Kia. I spent the entire first year of my marriage feeling guilty that Leo wasn't the first person I ran to with my problems. And even when I did confide in him, he wasn't always the person that made me feel better. A soul mate is someone who gets you. Someone you can tell anything to. I finally realized Leo was brought into my life to be my husband, my business partner, and my lover. The soul mate position had already been filled . . . by you."

I feel myself getting a little teary-eyed. "That is the sweetest thing you've ever said to me."

"I wasn't saying it to be sweet, Kia. I just want you to be happy, and if Flash can play a part in that . . ."

"Enough about Flash already."

"It's not like you've been dating much since you two split."

"Have you really forgotten what it's like out there, Di? I'm not young enough, hoochie enough, or needy enough for the average L.A. brotha. And frankly, I didn't hold out this long to end up with average, anyway. I want what you and Mom have."

"And what's that?"

"A guy who captures my heart as well as my imagination."

A slight blush crept across her face. "And Flash can't do that?"

"Half the time when he talks, Di, my eyes glaze over. It's the same with him. I'll mention something about work and he goes into a dead zone."

"I hear you, but I still say you're hung up on him."

"I wish people would stop saying that."

"Maya feels the same way, huh?"

"Probably. But actually I was talking about Drew."

"The guy from work?"

I nod. "I don't know how else to explain it except to say . . . imagine it's your birthday and a waiter offers you a slice of someone else's cake—would you eat it?"

"Chocolate cake from Rosebud? Heck, yeah," Diane said, licking her lips.

"Flash is someone else's chocolate cake. I'm just grubbing on a slice till my very own double-layered one arrives. So, you see, I'm not still hung up on Flash; I'm just in the mood for a little dessert."

Diane stared at me, almost searing a hole through my forehead.

"What?" I asked.

She stared at me harder. "Cough it up."

I guess we really are soul mates. She can see right through me.

"I asked him to go with me yesterday. He turned me down flat."

"Oooh. That sucks."

"So trust me when I say that whatever I was feeling, or thought I was feeling, I'm not feeling anymore."

"That's your ego talking, Kia. Not your heart."

I gave her a defiant *whatever* shoulder shrug.

Just then my dad popped his head into the room. At fifty-eight, he's still a looker. His dark skin is a bit weathered but not wrinkled. He's all salt and pepper now but most of his 'fro is still intact.

Growing up, I remember, most kids were afraid of their dads and went to their mothers for permission to do things. Not so for us. Dad was the softy, and we took advantage of that whenever possible.

"Girls, you can't hide in here forever. I know, I've tried."

"We're planning a getaway. Do you wanna come?" I asked.

"Where to? Vegas? Cabo?" He seemed excited.

"We're thinking of going to Paris for my birthday."

The look on his face said I'd killed the joy.

"Kia, I don't like going to French restaurants. If you twist my arm, though, I might spring for two nights at a hotel as a birthday gift."

It always struck me as odd that my father, an aeronautical engineer for Boeing, had never been much of a traveler. With the rare exception, if he couldn't get there by car or cruise ship, he wasn't going. Maybe knowing how a plane actually works, knowing exactly how many things can go wrong, makes one less inclined to board one. Being scientifically and mechanically challenged, I have no problem jumping on a plane at a moment's notice; I just don't want to do it alone.

I kissed his sweet little forehead. "They just don't make them like you anymore, Daddy."

"The only thing special about me is the two of you," he said, with a wink. "Dinner is on the table. We better get moving."

Being dutiful daddy's little girls, we obediently followed him into the dining room.

"HEAVENLY FATHER, we thank you for the opportunity to gather together once again. Please continue to watch over our family, especially Leo . . ."

The four of us were gathered around a B Smith–inspired, burgundy-and-gold, perfectly (some might argue *overly*) set table, holding hands, as my mother performed her weekly pre-meal sermon. Saying grace used to fall under my father's domain, until Mrs. Manning told my mother she saw Diane and me sharing a beer in our backyard one Sunday afternoon. We were, respectively, ten and twelve at the time. That evening, as my father opened his mouth to bless the food, my mother pre-empted him. After thanking God for the nourishment that sat before us, she then asked him to give her the strength to raise two headstrong girls. Girls who lie (we denied it happened). Girls who steal (it was one of my father's beers). Girls who bring dishonor to their parents (Mrs. Manning catching us in the act was worse than the act itself). By the time she said "Amen," Diane and I had lost our appetites, and our desire to ever drink again. Going off to college, thankfully, changed that, but Lorna's penchant for seizing the moment to express her concern or disappointment with our lives didn't.

"Help him regain his strength soon so that he and Diane can start working on giving me a grandchild."

Diane gave my hand a *Can you believe her?* squeeze.

"And, Lord, please help Kia find a man who will love and care for her in the way that she deserves."

I breathed a sigh of relief. That wasn't so bad. It was kind of sweet, actually. After all, that's what I wanted for myself.

"Help her to see that the fairy tale isn't going to happen. There is no such thing as a Prince Charming or a perfect man."

Diane squeezed my hand again.

I never said I wanted the fairy tale or the perfect man. I'm just looking for a brotha who can help pay the bills and give it to me good three times a week. *Oops, sorry, Lord*, I said to the man upstairs.

"Keep us in your grace until we are able to gather together once again. We ask that you do this in the name of the Father, the Son, and the Holy Ghost."

The four of us said, "Amen."

"You know, Lorna, just once it would be nice to start a meal with a simple 'God is great, God is good, let us thank him for our food,'" Daddy said.

In unison, Diane and I said a second "Amen."

DIANE LEFT EARLY to play Florence Nightingale to Leo, leaving me to battle with a kitchen full of dirty dishes and my mother alone.

"So, Europe, huh?" my mother said, dumping a stack of plates into the sink for me to wash. Since she insists that we each use a separate plate for salad, dinner, and dessert, the stack is towering over me like Lisa Leslie.

"I figured since I had all this vacation time coming, why not do something special for my birthday?"

"If special is what you're going for, the Congressional Black Caucus is meeting that weekend. You could stay with your cousin, Valerie. She and Marc have a beautiful home just outside the city."

"I'd rather let Diane clean my teeth with this," I said, holding up a dried macaroni-and-cheese-encrusted fork. D.C. in

August is muggy and miserable, and the same goes for my cousin Valerie.

"D.C. is a lovely city. You could shop and sightsee, soak up history and culture just as you could in Europe."

"Mom, D.C. is three hundred years old and Athens is, like, three thousand. Not exactly an apple-to-apple comparison."

"That may be, but D.C. has something Europe doesn't— eligible black men."

"I've been to the Caucus before and it wasn't all that. Most of the men were only eligible for the weekend. Come Monday, they suddenly remember they're married."

I knew this would shut her down. Lorna does not play the mistress game.

"I don't know why you just can't be happy for me, Mom. I'm going to Europe. Someplace you've never been. Isn't that what parents are supposed to want for their kids? To do more and to have more than they did?"

Lorna suddenly got a look in her eye that worried me. "I've always wanted to go to Paris. But you know how your father hates to travel. Maybe I should join you girls . . ."

Oh. God. No! Going to Europe with my mother would be like going to the prom with your brother—just dead-ass wrong! First of all, she'll have her School Administrator hat on the entire time. Ordering Di and me around, turning everything we do into an educational experience. And when she's not doing that, she'll put on her Susie Homemaker apron and critique the cleanliness and quality of service of every place we visit. It's not that my mother doesn't know how to have fun, it just never seems to happen when I'm anywhere in the vicinity.

"You would really leave Daddy here, all alone, for two whole weeks?" I said with as much dramatic flair as I could muster.

"You're right, the man would be lost with out me. I'd come

home and find he'd burned the house down trying to make toast. Oh well . . ." she said with a sigh. "It was a nice thought."

I suddenly felt like the grinch who stole Christmas. My father's aversion to travel has come at my mother's expense. A trip like this would be a dream come true for her. How can I stand in the way of that?

"You don't have to come for the whole trip, Mom. You could just meet up with us for a long weekend. I'm sure Dad can make do for a few days."

"To go all that way for just a weekend seems so extravagant. Besides, school starts back up the following week, there'll be so much for me to do. We're finally getting new books for two of our schools. No, you girls go on ahead and enjoy yourselves. I'll hold down the fort here."

I breathed a huge sigh of relief as my mother gave me a hug. Whenever we embrace I'm always struck by how petite and bony she is. The way she imposes her will on those she loves you'd expect her to be bigger. In my mind's eye, she was six feet tall, weighed two hundred and fifty pounds, with a booming voice. Yet everything about Lorna Carson, physically, is faint. Her skin tone, her fine hair, her mannered, soft-spoken voice. Even her wrinkles which, much to her chagrin, have started to take root around the corners of her light brown eyes and dainty mouth.

"Kia, five minutes ago you asked why I couldn't just be happy for you. Honey, I am happy for you. And I do want you to do things I've never done. But when I look back over my life, the thing that brings me the most joy is my family—my husband of thirty-six years and my two healthy, beautiful, successful daughters. I want that for you, too."

"Me, too, Mom. But there's a chance it might not work out that way. And I have to find a way to be okay with that. And your little digs don't help."

"What digs?"

I mimicked my mother's prayer. "Oh, Lord, please help Kia see that the fairy tale isn't going to happen. Please help her see that she should just latch on to the next bozo who comes along."

My mother put her hand on her hip in a dramatic fashion. "Kia, I said no such thing!"

"That's the implication, Mom. That I should lower my standards."

My mother began drying as I continued to wash. Her tiny hands, charted by narrow blue veins, moved at twice the speed of mine. "Well, dating that Flash person was proof you've already done that."

I took the dis in stride. I knew going in she wouldn't like the boy. She'd never been a fan of creative types. It's why after first encouraging my love for sewing, she withdrew her support when she realized I was considering going to the Fashion Institute instead of to a proper college. She let me know in no uncertain terms, if I continued to pursue a career in design I would be doing so without financial support from her or my father. Since all is fair in love and war, I acquiesced and went to the University of Southern California, one of the most expensive colleges in the country. One kick in the shin deserves another. At least, that's what Lorna always taught me. She may look like a soft brown mouse, but pull on her tail and she becomes a roaring, man-eating lion.

My mother takes my chin into her hands, forcing me to look at her. My attention is immediately drawn to her mouth. Even after a three-course meal, her lips are still a dewy Fashion Fair pink. My nude Chanel lip-gloss didn't last past my second sip of wine. I've been trying to lick moisture back into them ever since.

"Baby, I don't want you to lower your standards. I just want you to be happy."

Diane said that exact thing to me earlier tonight. Am I giving off some unhappy vibe I'm not aware of? Or do women who have a man blindly assume it simply because I don't?

"Wait till I tell Dotty my girls are going to Europe. She was going on the other day about Julie taking her kids to Disneyworld, like it was some big deal. Make sure you take lots of pictures with that fancy digital camera of yours. Julie used a disposable one and her pictures were nothing special."

I've always admired that about my mother, her ability to turn the details of my life into one-up-them points in hers.

Eight

Even disasters—there are always disasters when
you travel—can be turned into adventures.
—*Marilyn French, American author*

"TO WHAT DO I OWE this pleasant surprise?" I asked.

Guy was in court wrapping up a trial and Drew was out
questioning witnesses in preparation for one. It was one of the
rare times I had the office to myself, and I was not thrilled
about now having to entertain an uninvited guest. Harrison
McKinney was standing in my doorway looking like a man on
a mission. A man with tits on a mission.

"I was hoping I could appeal to that tiny heart of yours I
know is beating somewhere inside your chest," Harrison said
entering my office. "Kia, you're not seriously going to recom-
mend to Judge Powell that Terry Lewis serve the maximum
sentence. You're supposed to be one of the good guys."

"Yeah, and I proved it when I kicked the other kid's case
down to juvie. And got my ass chewed out by my boss for the
trouble," I replied.

Harrison was the opposing counsel on the juvenile assault
case I had just won. The one I'd begged Drew to take off my
hands. For me, this case highlighted everything that was wrong
with our judicial system.

Thanks to several blows to the head, the twenty-five-year-old white male victim now suffers from chronic memory loss and thus doesn't remember getting the shit beaten out of him by an unknown number of YBMs. Nothing more descriptive than that, just YBMs. Young. Black. Males.

That was enough for the LAPD to round up seventeen of them; a room full of Shamar Moore to Morris Chestnut look-alikes. And damn if dumb luck didn't piss in their lap. The SOBs actually netted one of the perps.

With no physical evidence linking him to the crime, if fourteen-year-old Jamal Greene had kept his mouth shut, the police would still be combing the streets for YBMs and he'd be out somehwere enjoying his summer break before starting high school.

Upon his arrest, Jamal immediately asked to see his mother. The police called her at home, knowing damn well a single mother of three would be at work. Waiting for her shift to end would give them time to work Jamal over. Not physically, just mind games.

It didn't take long before Jamal admitted to being present when his friend, Terry, stole the watch off a guy lying in an alley. Judging from the amount of blood oozing from the back of his head, they thought the victim was dead.

Within the hour Terry was arrested and charged with aggravated assault. Never mind the victim couldn't pick the boys out of a lineup. Never mind the defendant is nearly two inches shorter than the victim making it highly unlikely that he'd be able to strike the victim on the top of the head, as the medical examiner's report stated.

Jamal's confession placed them at the scene of the crime. Terry being caught with the victim's watch in his possession gave him motive. It took the jury less than four hours to come back with a guilty verdict.

"Kia, it's bad enough the boy has to do time in a man's prison. But twenty years? For essentially stealing a sixty-dollar watch?"

"Guilt trip me all you want, Harrison, but my hands are tied. Holden doesn't want the DA's office to appear soft on crime. He wants blood. It's not going to be my proudest moment, but, yes, I will be asking for the maximum penalty."

"Assuming he survives, he'll be thirty-five when he gets out. What kind of sense does that make?"

"None. But it's the law," I said flatly.

I used to believe in the law. Not so much in the practice of it, that's all about manipulation—manipulating the judge, the jury, whoever stands in the way of your getting what you want—but in the fundamentals of it. If A, then B. If you murder someone, you go to jail. If you sell drugs, you go to jail. These are concepts I understand.

A funny thing happens, though, when the law meets up with racism and poverty. The absolutes become maybes, sometimes, almost nevers.

If you sell crack, you go to jail. If you sell cocaine, you might not. Black men sell crack. White boys sell cocaine. You do the math.

"I hope you can sleep at night, Kia. You know, if Terry were white we wouldn't be having this conversation."

I knew all too well. If you're a *group* of underage white boys who get caught *joy riding* in a car that *doesn't belong to you,* your private attorney will see to it that you never serve any jail time. Your parents will pay a fine and you will perform a hundred hours of community service. A slap on the wrist.

If you're a *gang* of underage black kids and the police catch you *driving* a *stolen* car, your court-appointed attorney will do his best to plea-bargain your case down to a misdemeanor, meaning you'll do two to three years. A slap in the face.

These truths I hold to be self-evident. And it pisses me off.

"A lot of my cases keep me up at night, Harrison. I hate putting brothas in jail that don't belong there. And every chance I get to cut one of them a break, I do it. This is just not one of those times. I'm sorry. I saved Jamal. I can't save everybody."

"I'm not asking you to save anybody, Kia. I'm just asking you to do the right thing."

Harrison grabbed his briefcase. "You know . . . I have the perfect cure for your sleep troubles." He flashed a sweet, double-chin smile. "Me."

No, he didn't just walk into my office begging for a kid's life and walk out begging for some bootie. Brothas. You gotta love them.

"You still seeing your mystery man?" he inquired.

I didn't have the heart to tell Harrison I didn't want to go out with him because he needed to wear a bra. Instead I opted for a junior high move and told him I had a man. I don't know what's worse, the fact that I don't have a man or the fact that I lied about it?

"We're hanging in there. You know how it is," I replied.

"Yeah, I know exactly how it is."

His tone suggested he was on to my lie. He's probably heard the *Thanks but I have a man* line a thousand times. He and I both knew it was rarely the truth. Every time I lock a brotha up or Harrison fails to set one free, that's one more black woman who'll sit home alone on a Friday night.

"See you in court, Counselor," he said.

As he walked out the door I felt bad having denied both his requests, but what's a girl to do? I stared at my shoes. It's what I do when my thoughts outweigh the solutions. Via Spiga open-toe pumps. White. It's okay . . . it's June. I see that Nancy (her real name is Pheng Suyen Lee, at least that's what it says on her cosmetology license) did a banging job on my pedicure. It's been two weeks and not a chip in sight. I looked up from my feet long enough to answer the ringing phone.

"Kia Carson."

"It's Barb. Are you ready to purchase your plane tickets to-day as we discussed? Today is the absolute last day I can hold them at the quoted price."

Barb is the travel agent Drew had recommended. We were carrying on the most torrid love-hate relationship two straight women can have. I loved her when she scored great hotel rates. I hated her when she called to remind me I owed her more money.

"August is a busy travel month. God only knows what these tickets will cost tomorrow. That's if they're still available to-morrow," she continued.

Travel is Barb's life and she never lets you forget it. Come to think of it, travel had become my life as well.

Diane and I argued for a week about where to go. I was leaning toward Paris and Mykonos. Drew was always talking about how fantastic Greece is. Di wanted to go to London and the Netherlands, two places her husband had no desire to visit.

Barb helped us settle on London and Paris. The two cities providing the perfect balance of culture, shopping, and dining. A well-rounded vacation, by all accounts.

"Barb, I'll call you back on a three-way before the end of the day."

"Call before five or these last few weeks of planning have been for naught. Ta," Barb said before hanging up.

I would've bought my ticket a week ago but Diane gave me some song and dance about her credit-card billing cycle and needing to wait so the charge wouldn't hit until the following month. It sounded a bit janky to me, but whatever. It's do-or-die time now. I decided to call her at the office.

"Griggs' Dentistry, how may I help you?"

"Hey, Daria, it's Kia. Is Di free?"

"Yeah, hold on."

I sang along with 50 Cent to the radio hold music. I love black-owned businesses.

"Um, she must've stepped out for a minute. Can she call you back?"

Something in Daria's voice struck me as off. I pressed her. "Where'd she go?"

"I don't know. But I'll have her call you when she returns." Click.

I stared at the phone in disbelief. Did that heifer just hang up on me?

I knew there was no way Diane stepped out without telling anyone where she was going at eleven in the morning on a Friday. Something was up. I called back.

"Griggs' Dentistry, how may I help you?"

"Yeah, you can get Diane on the phone."

"Um, Kia, I just told you—"

"Daria, you're doing what she told you to do, I get it. But folks are trying to get a three-day weekend any way they can, even if it means going to the dentist. Fridays are her money days and she's there making as much of it as she can. So. Put. Her. Ass. On. The. Phone."

Daria put me on hold. Mary J. was crooning about being in love. Whatever.

Diane got on the phone full of attitude. "What is so damn urgent, Kia?"

"You know good and well we have to buy our plane tickets today."

"Look, Kia. I don't know how to tell you this. But . . . I can't go."

I was hotter than July. "Excuse me?"

"The good news is you're going to be an auntie!"

I felt a blood vessel burst inside my head. I searched for the right words. I'm the big sister. I'm supposed to have all the answers. All the words of wisdom.

"Kia, are you still there?"

"Congratulations. Mom will be thrilled." It was the best I could do.

"We can go to Europe next year. I promise," Diane said.

That was the last thing I wanted to hear.

"I was looking forward to going as much as you were, Kia. This really caught us by surprise. I waited so long to tell you because I didn't believe it. When my period didn't come I thought it was just my body getting used to being off the pill. I mean, we've only been really trying for a few months."

Figures. Infertility is rampant in the over-thirty set and she gets pregnant on a whim. I knew I was being a bitch. This should be a happy time. So what if I'm going to be an aunt before I'm a wife? So what if I'm going to become the sole focus of my mother's disappointment? (Being a successful attorney means nothing to her without a husband and kids to share it with.) So fucking what! I could handle it.

"Di, I'm tickled pink, really. You are going to be a great mom. And I can't wait to be an auntie. I love you. See you on Sunday."

I hung up, not feeling good about what just happened, or for what was about to happen. I had to call Barb and tell her we weren't going and listen to her whine and complain about how much of her time I've wasted.

We'll go to Europe next year. Yeah, right. Next year it'll be something else. They're buying a new house. They're having another baby.

Maya will have a job by then. Her boss probably won't let her take the time off. Maybe her boyfriend, Aaron, will have proposed and she'll be in the throes of wedding plans. I just needed to face facts. I was never going to Europe. I was never going anywhere.

I put my head down on the desk.

"What's wrong? You missed the Barney's Warehouse sale?" I heard Drew say from the doorway.

"Judging from that hideous tie you're wearing, I'd say so did you."

There was nothing wrong with his tie. I just felt like being evil.

"Who pissed in your Cheerios?"

"My sister can't go to Europe."

"So?"

"So, now I don't have anybody to go with."

"So?"

"So now I'm not going!" I said, utterly frustrated with him, my sister, my life.

"What are you, twelve? It's not like you're traveling to war-torn Bosnia or Afghanistan, Carson. You can go to Europe by yourself. I do it all the time."

"I know I can. I just don't want to."

"Fine. Call Barb and have her arrange another one of your all-inclusive resort vacations. You know—where the only locals you meet are the waiters. And in between massages and karaoke, you can mingle with other whiny unhappy single women just like yourself. Gee, that sounds sort of like what you do when you're not on vacation."

Ouch! That wasn't very nice. True, but not very nice. Yes, I sort of live in a cocoon. And, yes, it would be nice to break out of it a little. But Europe? By myself? Naw, I'm not really feel-ing that, either.

"Don't you have some cases you should be out there losing?" I asked.

Drew settled into his chair, putting his feet up on his desk. "Nope."

As I went back to staring at my shoes, I heard Drew making phone calls. Realizing I couldn't put off Barb forever, I did the same.

"Hey, Barb, it's Kia."

She exhaled dramatically before speaking. "So what's it going to be?"

"Um, I uh, well, uh . . ."

"You're not going, are you, Kia?"

I found the resolve in her voice irritating. I turned my back to Drew and whispered into the phone, praying he couldn't hear me.

"Yes, I am. But Diane won't be joining me, so you may have to downscale the hotel reservations. But room service and decent sheets are still crucial. Oh, and you might as well look into Greece. If I'm going to do this, I might as well go all out."

"You won't believe this, but I just found a dirt-cheap package for another client flying into Athens for a day and then on to Mykonos for a week."

"Fine. You have my AmEx number. Can you make all the arrangements and fax me a finalized itinerary by the end of the day?"

"Well, of course I can. It's just . . . what . . . what happened to Diane?"

"Life happened to Diane."

Her silence said she wanted to hear more.

"She and her husband are expecting, so Europe's on hold. For her. But not for me. I can't tell you how many concerts I've missed out on because I couldn't find anyone to go with. How many fantastic restaurants have opened and closed without me getting to experience them? I'm grown. I should be able to do things by myself. Right?"

"I prefer it, actually. No one else's needs to consider. No one else's agenda to comply with," Barb said reassuringly.

"Exactly," I said, not so assuredly.

Afraid I might change my mind, I quickly hung up. My heart was pounding. I spun my chair back around and caught Drew smiling at me. He undoubtedly heard every word.

"Get that stupid smirk off your face. My going to Europe has nothing to do with you. Barb put a lot of time and effort into this trip and I didn't have the heart to cancel on her," I explained.

Drew's laugh told me he didn't believe a word of it, but that was the least of my worries. I'd just booked an extensive solo trip to Europe. I felt like an oaf who's just woken up from a drunken stupor and discovered that I've enlisted in the army.

FUUUCK!!!!

En Route

Nine

No matter where you go—there you are.
—*Earl MacRauch, American author*

TWO HOURS into a ten-hour flight and sleep is about as far from me as London. I wasn't kidding when I said my day wasn't going well. Terry Lewis was sentenced to ten years in prison today. If he stays out of trouble, he could get away with serving five. He'll be twenty years old when he gets out, too young to drink a celebratory beer but old enough to have his life ruined. Not ruined enough for the DA, though. It wasn't enough that I sent him to jail. I was supposed to keep him there.

I did not seek the maximum penalty as ordered. It seems I did have a heart beating quietly inside me after all. And my boss was not happy about it.

"Close the damn door," Holden said gruffly.

Any illusions I had that I might escape my summons to his office with all my limbs intact died on the spot. I knew I would take some heat for my decision, but I had never seen Holden so livid.

"Ms. Carson, did I or did I not advise you as to how I wanted this case to go down?"

I gave a sheepish nod. "For what it's worth, I consulted with the victim, and he was fine with my recommendation. He's not so sure Terry Lewis is the one who bashed his head in."

"You don't work for the victims, Ms. Carson. You work for me."

I had no comeback for that one, so I held my tongue.

"What exactly are you going to say to Joe Citizen when he's car-jacked by a kid just released from prison after serving a bullshit stint courtesy of your incompetence?"

"Sir, if Terry Lewis grows up to be a car-jacker, it's because that's all prison taught him to be."

"I expected contrite, Ms. Carson, not glib. You've just made this a helluva lot easier. Consider yourself suspended."

My whole world goes black. I try to shake off the nausea that wells up inside of me. Suspended? People who fuck up get suspended. I didn't fuck up. I did the right the thing. The just thing.

"Excuse me, sir? I don't think I heard you," I managed to say.

"The good news is your suspension will run concurrent with your vacation. But it still goes as a black mark in your file."

I was speechless. The only words that did come to mind, I had no business saying.

"If this were the first time, I might've excused your blatant disregard of my order. But I've reviewed your file and it seems this is a pattern with you, Ms. Carson. A pattern that stops today."

Holden dramatically tossed my file onto his desk. "Time after time you've gone for the minimum penalty when it's department policy to go for the max. You plead out or dismiss cases that should be tried with both guns blazing. And rumor has it the Public Defender's office looks forward to going up against you in court. They've pegged you for a softy."

"I beg to differ. No one looks forward to going up against me in court because they tend to lose. Yes, I weed out a lot of bullshit cases, but when I take one to trial, I win. My file should also show that I've got one of the strongest conviction rates in the entire office."

"We answer to the people, Ms. Carson. And the people don't want weeding."

"Our mandate isn't to serve the people, sir. It's to make sure justice is served. At least that's what they taught us in law school."

I'm not endearing myself to this man in any way. Being right at this point isn't the same as being smart.

"You're not in law school anymore, Dorothy. I suggest that while you're out on your suspension, you think long and hard about your future here. This is a wake-up call. I've seen glimpses of your talent. Learn to play by my rules and I'll reward you for it. Continue to play by your own, and this will be the last pleasant conversation we ever have. Enjoy your trip."

I walked out of his office wishing a giant earthquake would hit L.A. and a sinkhole would swallow me up. With that thought in my head, and anxiety rumbling in my belly, I raced off to my hair appointment.

I PUSH the attendant button. I'm going to need a lot more alcohol if I'm going to shake off my work blues.

"More champagne?" Karin asks.

I hold out my empty glass a little too eagerly.

"You're not a sloppy drunk, are you?"

"Probably. But I never let it get that far."

Karin pours me a full glass. "A crybaby *and* a control freak. I'm sure the blokes are lining up."

I do a quick ring check. Only a single woman can say something crazy like that to me and not get a beat down. Yep, her third finger is as unadorned as mine.

"The fact that I'm a sex goddess certainly helps," I say, taking a healthy gulp.

Karin glances at the *Fodor's Travel Guide* that lies on my tray. "Please tell me you're not going to reduce exploring my country to what you find in that dreary book?"

"You mean Charles Dickens' house isn't a must-see?"

"If you're an eighty-year-old anglophile."

"So what *are* the must-see places of London?"

"Paris," she says with a hearty laugh. "Tell you what..." Karin writes her number on the inside of my travel guide. I make every attempt to ignore the fact that my property has just been defaced.

"I've got three days off later in the week. Ring me and we'll meet for drinks. Most of my friends are on holiday and I detest imbibing alone."

"What holiday is it?"

"You Yanks call it a vacation."

Ah, my first lesson in British-speak. I feel so Continental.

"Shall I ring you anon?" I ask.

"Not if you're going to be talking like that. What are you, some sort of Shakespeare buff?"

"Nope. Reruns of *Frasier*."

Karin laughs at me and heads off to pour a glass of champagne for 6E.

London

Ten

> Travel is more than the seeing of sights; it is a change that goes on, deep and permanent, in the ideas of living.
>
> —*Miriam Beard, American author*

AT EXACTLY 11:30 A.M. every other day from August to March, excluding bad-weather days, it happens. The Buckingham Palace guards. And the changing of them. I initially thought it was going to be corny, but it was actually pretty cool.

Extremely British in nature. All pomp, all circumstance. Not to mention the tall black furry hats. With background music provided by a live band, the New Guard marches from their barracks down Birdcage Walk as the Old Guard marches up from St. James's Palace. They meet in front of the palace gates, giving each other dap, symbolically representing the turning over of keys. And just like that, a new shift begins.

Instead of stealing ideas for TV shows—e.g., *American Idol*—we should import this tradition. Imagine a trip to Wal-Mart if such a thing happened every eight hours.

Having enjoyed the outside festivities so much, I nix my plan to visit the Royal Ceremonial Dress Collection at Kensington Palace, where many of Princess Di's gowns are housed, and decide instead to take a look-see inside Buckingham Palace. For eleven pounds, roughly nineteen dollars U.S., I, along with thirty-nine other foreign visitors, am given an official tour by Prudence, our perfectly proper, ghostly pale tour guide.

"This six-hundred-room estate was purchased by King George III in 1762 for his wife, Charlotte," Prudence informs the group.

Putting the date into context with the limited amount of American history I have retained since graduating high school, I realize that King George III is the king who lost the colonies. A detail Prudence has managed to gloss over as she takes us through the throne room.

Standing before a portrait of George and Charlotte, she continues our history lesson: "As was the practice back then, it was an arranged marriage. In fact, the two did not meet until September 9, 1761—their wedding day. It was anything but love at first sight, as the King was greatly underwhelmed with Charlotte's rather pedestrian features . . ."

As she resumes walking, the group following close behind, I pause to get a better look at the portrait and something strikes me as odd. As a whole, the English are frightfully pale people. So much so that I'm almost tempted to say that I've never seen a *white* person until I came here. If *Caucasian* weren't such a mouthful to say, I would never again call the nonblack people back home *white* after seeing the English. It's why after studying the portrait further, I find myself disrupting the tour.

"Excuse me, but is this the Queen Charlotte you've been talking about?" I say pointing to the portrait.

"Yes," Prudence replies.

"The pedestrian-looking one the King wasn't really feeling, though he must've got over it since they went on to have fifteen children?"

"Yes," she says with more than a slight amount of annoyance.

"This babe isn't pedestrian, she's black!" I exclaim.

The entire group gasps.

I continue, "I mean, you're going on and on about how Charlotte is responsible for bringing about the tradition of decorating Christmas trees. And how one of her birthday parties is the inspiration behind the debutante balls high society still holds to this day. But you didn't mention nary a word about her being black!"

I wouldn't have believed it was possible but at this Prudence becomes another shade whiter, turning almost a pale blue. And while her mouth remains closed, her eyes have a serious look of denial about them, spurring me to present my case as if in court.

"Look at her coloring. She's damn near a Hershey's Kiss compared to her husband. And look at her nose. It's as wide as Asia!"

Thirty-nine sets of feet scamper back over to me and the portrait. Two African women push their way to the front of the group, nearly knocking over a Japanese couple in order to get a better look. Amid the group's yeas and nays, and various other comments, the tour guide tries to explain.

"It, it, is no secret . . ." Prudence struggles to find the right words. "That due to calculated and frequent interbreeding many European bluebloods can trace their roots back to Margarita de Castro y Sousa, a Moorish branch of the Portuguese aristocracy."

Translation: Sistagirl was black.

"I don't know how it works over here, but across the pond, one drop makes you black."

"While Queen Charlotte was a direct descendant of Margarita, she technically would be considered a quadroon," Prudence says with more attitude than necessary. Especially since the prosecutor in me never really goes on vacation.

"So, technically, since the throne is passed down through lineage, logic would follow that the current Queen of England,

Elizabeth, is a direct descendant of Charlotte, and therefore is more likely than not walking around with that one drop I'm talking about..."

All eyes of various shapes and colors fall upon Prudence who, by the look on her face, wishes she had called in sick today.

"So it would seem," she manages to say. "Now, if there are no further interruptions, I'd like to continue on with the appointed tour."

As the group trots off behind her, I take one last deep look into Charlotte's eyes and feel something stir inside me I had never felt before.

Knowing Charlotte existed means I've still got a shot. Face it, little black girls might play princess—plenty of them dressed up as Sleeping Beauty last Halloween—but we don't grow up believing we can really become one.

And nobody dreams about becoming an African princess. It may not be politically correct, but it's nonetheless true. African princesses don't wear crowns. They may produce the world's shiniest diamonds, but they don't wear them in tiaras and parade around the way white princesses do. They don't have footmen or carriages or televised weddings, either. What's the point of being a princess if you don't get any of the perks?

Then there's *Shrek*, an animated movie about a troll princess. A troll princess! Disney and the like would rather spend millions of dollars making a movie about an ugly, green, snaggle-toothed Royal Highness than make one about a black, brown, red, or yellow one. And *Mulan* and *Pocahontas* don't count. Those girls were working-class hos. Not a ball gown or throne in sight.

As Prudence drones on and on about the ornate nineteenth-century architecture, the skillfully hidden doorways, the Portland stone façade, it occurs to me that the Brits are missing out on a golden opportunity. If they really wanted to set this tour off, they'd let visitors dress in period costume and then walk around the joint. I'd cough up an extra ten pounds or so for the chance to do some authentic role playing. I'd kick in a twenty if they'd let me wear a tiara.

All right, I confess, my mother's dinnertime prayer wasn't completely off the mark. There is a minute, that last minute before I drift off to sleep every night, when I imagine that he comes. Prince Charming, that is. Not the perfect man, but one who loves you despite your flaws, whatever they may be—your bizarre sleeping habits, your passive-aggressive relationship with your evil stepmother, your obsession with midgets. The minute doesn't last long enough for me to see his face. I just know that he comes. And I'm always happy to see him, although I can't quite shake the feeling that he's not really there to see me. Knowing Charlotte existed means hell yeah he's there to see me. And why shouldn't he be? I'm as worthy of a *Her Royal Highness* title as anyone else. I don't care what Walt Disney or this stupid tour guide says.

Eleven

A traveler without knowledge is a bird without wings.

—*Sa'di, Persian poet*

THE STREET OF CHANGING SEASONS. In the movie *Notting Hill*, there's this really cool scene where the seasons change from a warm sunny spring to a frosty wet winter. All of this happens as Hugh Grant, in a total funk because his girl, Julia Roberts, has dogged him, walks down the street.

At the time I thought it was no big deal that an Englishman walks down the same street for an entire year and doesn't come across any black people. I mean, it happens all the time in Woody Allen movies. But through a quick search on the hotel's lobby Internet system, I learned that Notting Hill wasn't much of a neighborhood until the West Indians made it one.

Hitler's war had taken a heavy toll and England was in serious need of a strong male workforce. Folklore has it King George VI sent a call out to his Caribbean royal subjects, suggesting that the streets of Britain were paved with gold. London was soon flooded with Antiguans, Bajans, Jamaicans, and Trinidadians eager for a piece of the good life.

The new arrivals quickly discovered that British streets were only paved with golden potholes. A colored workforce might be needed, but it's rarely wanted. Finding work was easy, finding a place to live, though, was harder to come by. Britain was the mother country but she was only offering love and comfort to her white children, forcing the Jamaicans to settle en masse in Brixton and Tottenham, while the Bajans and the Trinis headed for Notting Hill.

And even though Hugh Grant doesn't see any black faces in his yearlong sojourn (not even Tina Turner, who is a well-known fixture in this community), I, thankfully, am seeing more than a few. Not as many as there once were. Now that the West Indians have made it a decent place to live, their white countrymen are taking it back.

It's a lovely August day, by English standards, anyway. Gray but not raining. It's about twenty-one degrees Celsius. That's seventy-one degrees Fahrenheit. Winter weather for a California girl, but a day at the beach for Londoners.

I am appropriately dressed for this so-called summer day: a white linen Burberry trench, a pair of Brazilian bootie-hugging jeans, and a French-cuffed dress shirt. I found the most adorable, old-fashioned red-telephone-booth cuff links yesterday on my shopping expedition to Harrods and I just had to wear them today. Having worn cute but not walking-friendly navy Charles David spectator pumps, I'm copping a squat and people-watching outside of George's Portobello Fish Bar, while grubbing on fish-and-chips.

I spot a hundred-and-fifty-pound Saint Bernard walking a hundred-pound whisper of a woman. The dog enjoys the stroll, rarely missing an opportunity to gnaw on plants, sniff out a cute little bitch, or receive a friendly pat from a passerby. His owner, though, is bored by it all and clearly wants to get the experience over with as quickly as possible.

What a shame. This place is oozing atmosphere: arty types mingle with Rastafarians who mingle with Trustafarians (rich, white, British brats).

The "Hill" is a multicultural mecca, where trendy little specialty shops abut fashionable bistros and posh antique markets. What's not to love? The dog gets it—why doesn't she?

Her fashionable wide-leg gray slacks, along with her extremely pointy-toed camel flats and face-flattering bob haircut, tell me she's clearly a woman of privilege. She probably lives in an adorable flat close by, adorned in the requisite shabby-chic-meets-English-country décor. It's midday on a Friday and she's not at work. Life can't be all that bad. So what's with the dulled expression, I wonder?

It hits me that someone could observe the same about me. Speeding to work in my convertible Audi, dressed to thrill but not a smile in sight. Looking at my British dog-walking counterpart makes me wonder: If looking great and living great aren't the key to happiness, what is?

Maybe it isn't about waiting for something to catch you by surprise, but just remaining open to it. The dog walker appears to me to be as open as Macy's on Christmas Day.

"Didn't your mum teach you it's not polite to stare?"

Oh my God! The boy is fine. Not my usual flow, with his light skin, long dreads, and slender build. But, like I said, he's fiiine!

"She taught me it was bad form to get caught staring."

He laughs. "Touché."

He's not wearing a ring. He's damn right touché.

"She also warned me not to talk to strangers."

"Smart woman." He tips his head at me and walks inside the restaurant.

Shit! What just happened? He flirted. Then I flirted. And then he walked away? That's not how it's supposed to go. That's *not* how it's supposed to go!

I replay the exchange in my head again. He said . . . then I said . . . then he walked away. What the . . . ?

Maybe it's my breath. I blow into my hand and smell. Dear God it smells of tartar sauce. A definite turn-off. But he can't possibly hold that against me. I'm at a fish market, for goodness sakes. Being peppermint fresh really isn't an option here.

Maybe he doesn't like my braids. I still haven't decided if I like my braids. He might be an anti-fake-hair-even-the-expensive-kind kind of guy. Upset by our all-too-brief exchange, I shove a huge piece of fish into my mouth and chomp away.

"I'm Derrick, by the way."

An open hand waits for mine. He came back. The beautiful dreaded brotha came back!

I'm able to complete the handshake (buttery soft hands, obviously not a working-class man) but not the verbal part of the introduction. My vocal cords are currently blocked by chunks of battered fish smothered in tartar sauce. My mum/mother also warned me not to eat like a pig in public. When will I learn she might be right about a few things?

Derrick, catching it all, patiently waits for me to swallow. In my hurry to do so, I practically bruise my throat causing me to sound like a drag queen.

"Kia."

"Mind if I join you?"

Okay, so it's not just baritone voices that turn me on—accents work, too.

"Please do."

"If people-watching is your thing, you'll have to come back for the Bank Holiday. They'll be queueing everywhere."

I laugh. "We love to que."

Derrick looks slightly confused.

"Black people and bar-b-que. We're always ready to fire it up," I add.

I've obviously made a huge faux pas because Derrick is laughing hysterically.

"Ah—when *we* queue, we line up. They'll be tons of people lined up in the streets."

It's official. I am an idiot. I rummage through my brain trying to find anything that will prove otherwise.

"Two million strong, I hear. The largest cultural festival in Europe. Complete with floats, elaborate costumes, and steel pan bands."

He seems impressed. "An informed American, what can be sexier than that?"

"A kind Brit, I'd say. Equally hard to come by."

We share a smile that lingers in the air like expensive perfume.

"How much longer can the Commonwealth expect to enjoy your company?"

Again, I search my brain for just the right thing to say, something clever and flirty.

"Long enough to get into a little bit of trouble, I hope."

I notice a slight gleam in his eye. Bingo!

"Maybe I can help with that. Where are you staying?"

"The Millennium Knightsbridge."

Our moment is interrupted by a squeaky voice. "So sorry I'm late."

Before me now stands a beautiful dark-skinned woman/child with a perfectly coiffed wild afro. She kisses Derrick, the guy I was hoping would be my man for the next few days, first on his right cheek, then on his left.

"That's okay, love, Kia here has been keeping me company. Kia, this is Rita. Rita, this is our new American friend, Kia."

What's this *our* crap? I don't know her. This is apparently not a stumbling block for Rita, because before I know it, I'm right-cheeked then left-cheeked as well. Great. Miss Thing has fresh breath and silky smooth skin.

Rita cocks her head and winks at Derrick. "I love how you only make friends with the pretty girls."

She plops her cheery self into a chair and eats from his plate. I can see now that he has ordered enough food for two. Not a good sign. Although . . . while I was introduced as *friend* Kia, she was just plain old Rita. I remain cautiously optimistic.

"Has Derrick been grilling you about the States? We plan to travel there for our honeymoon."

Fiancée Rita. Shit!

"We didn't get that far. She's been dazzling me with her knowledge of our Carnival."

He really needs to stop smiling at me. It's that stupid smile that had me thinking I was possibly going to get my freak on later.

"A public nuisance, if you ask me. If it weren't for the delicious food stands, I wouldn't come at all," Rita says, mixing ketchup and tartar sauce together and slathering it on her chunky chips.

Great! Just what the world needs—another skinny girl who gets to eat like a wrestler. God is really testing me today, I see.

"Rita, how could you say such a thing? The Carnival isn't a food festival. It has a real historical significance," Derrick chastises.

Everything about Rita—the furrow in her brow, the vacant look in her eye, the downturn of her mouth—says she could give a flying fig. I, on the other hand, am eager to hear more.

"So what's the story behind the Carnival?"

"While you were having your race riots, we were having ours. Only difference being, black Americans burned down their own neighborhoods, and some Teddies came in and trashed ours."

"I'm guessing 'Teddy' is British slang for cracker?"

"In protest of the racism perpetrated against us, we began hosting the Carnival, sort of an ode to the one held in Trinidad, which marked the abolition of slavery," Derrick adds.

It amazes me that Muslims won't hesitate to strap a bomb to their chest and walk into a crowded square to voice their contempt for the system, but black people around the world believe they can solve all of their problems by simply marching in the streets. What is that about? I'm not an advocate of killing innocent people, but I'm not really sure how taking to the streets solves anything. The March on Washington and, later, the Million Man March, were symbolic gestures of humanity, but they did not evoke change. Boycotts evoke change. Lawsuits evoke change. Marching in the streets evokes traffic jams.

"Perhaps you could shed some light on something for me?" Derrick asks me.

"Fire away," I say while hating myself for wondering what it's like to hear a Brit talk dirty in bed.

"Don't Americans have a saying about not shitting where they eat? Why would blacks torch their own neighborhoods?"

"Maybe it's because the last time a large group of us ventured into a white neighborhood we ended up picking cotton for two hundred years?"

Derrick sits back in his seat, his eyes on mine. "We have to watch out for this one, Rita, she's rather cheeky."

If cheeky means pissed off you have a fiancée, then, yeah, that's what I am.

Derrick turns his body toward Rita but manages to keep his eyes on me. "Kia said she was looking to get into a little trouble. I thought she could come hang out with us tonight?"

Oh, he's good. He's real good.

Rita fixes her sweet brown eyes on me as well. "That would be lovely."

She places her delicate hand on top of what appears, by comparison, to be my manly hands.

"Do come. We promise to show you a brilliant time." She throws me the same head-cocked wink she gave Derrick.

Whoa! Is she coming on to me? Is this some threesome sort of thing? Oh, I could kill Diane for not being here right now. My puritan ass just wasn't built for this. I was all for checking things out with him, but now there's a her. A childhood song rings in my head. *No, no. Never, never. Uh, uh, uh.*

I rise from the table as quickly as I can. "I hate to cut this short, but I really have to go. I booked tea at the Ritz."

"Well, now you must absolutely join us tonight. A girl who does back-to-back meals I simply must know better," Rita squeals.

She really needs to be slapped. Like she can't see the slight pooch I've been trying to suck in ever since she sat her skinny freaky behind down. Back-to-back meals, puh-leeze.

I grab my coat. "It was nice meeting you both."

Derrick hands me his card. *Derrick Cummings, Professor of Music, New College.*

Damn! I'd always fantasized about sleeping with a professor. And every girl fantasizes about sleeping with a musician. *That's* the kind of twofer I had in mind.

"I wrote my mobile on the back. Ring us in a bit and we'll have settled on our plans. You'll be in good hands, I promise. We'll swing by your hotel to pick you up, so you won't have to worry about coming alone."

Swing by my hotel. I bet.

"Thanks, but I have to pass. I made plans to meet up with a friend tonight," I say.

"Is it an all-night friend, or just a meet-for-drinks friend?" Rita asks.

No, this heifer isn't trying to get all up in my business.

"If it's the former, surely you two can find some time to share a pint with us. If it's the latter, there's no reason why you can't meet up with us afterwards."

Oh, I've got a reason—YOU!

Rita leans over and double-kisses me goodbye. She smells the way a lot of young women do, like the perfume is wearing them. Derrick also gives me the European kiss, kiss. He smells like linen air-dried in the summer sun.

Yuck. I shouldn't be smelling him. I need to flee. I need to flee now. I'm half a block away when I turn around and spot Derrick lovingly nibbling on Rita's ear as if they were the only two people on the planet. Double yuck!

Twelve

"Afraid" is a country with no exit visa.
—*Audre Lorde, African-American poet*

I'M HAVING A BLOOD TRANSFUSION. I'm not exactly sure what it is, but I'm sucking it down as if my life depended on it.

Karin was kind enough to take me to a few authentic pubs, where locals like to end their workday drinking warm beer and eating dry crusty bread with crumbly cheese, while throwing darts and talking shit.

The talking shit part I enjoyed, but they can have the rest of it. Most pubs are short-staffed, so forget about a waitress coming to your table to take your order. It's a glimpse into the future these places want no part of.

The only upside to pubbing is that you don't have to tip the bartender. A welcome reprieve since essentially he's serving nothing but piss on tap. Britain's equivalent to an American icy cold one is a warm gassy brew they call *bitters*. It's disgusting. It's the real reason the Pilgrims fled to America. That and the depressing weather.

A true Brit would rather die than give up going to his favorite public house. But I'm finding one man's refuge is another man's torture chamber. Pubs are smoky, dark-wooded, spittle-stained dens where one is more likely to find a boar's head on the wall than, say, a sconce. I for one think a sconce can go a long way to adding a certain something to a room that a stuffed animal's head is simply incapable of doing. Clearly I'm in the minority on this, as pubs like The Lamb and Flag have been packing them in since the 1600s. Since you can't argue with history, the best I can hope for is that the experience doesn't make me bitter.

Thankfully, Karin is as particular as I am and finds pub life worthy of a giant snub.

We're now at a sexy little spot more suitable to both of our sensibilities. Pharmacy is a restaurant that pays homage to all things medicinal, in both its décor and its menu. Hence the blood transfusion. Hence the drunken smile on my face.

We've scored prime seats at the aspirin-shaped bar and we're sitting amongst a cross section of bankers, artists, posers, and tourists. This could be L.A., only no one has their eye on the door, in anticipation of a bigger name walking in. The patrons seem content to enjoy the company of whoever is in front of them.

"Thank you for bringing me here. I really needed this," I say, emptying my second drink.

"This being . . . ?"

"A twenty-dollar cocktail, in a swanky joint, where absolutely nobody knows my name."

"Anon . . . ymity is important to you, is it?" Karin is one transfusion ahead of me. And it's starting to show.

"Here I could be a twenty-eight-year-old third-grade virgin schoolteacher."

"That's what you'd hope to be?" The disdain in her voice comes across loud and clear.

"That's the beauty of it, Karin. I can change up whenever I like."

She waves to the hospital-scrub-wearing bartender, indicating we want another round. "Change up to something more festive. Virginity is so overrated."

An image of me sitting contentedly behind a sewing machine pops into my head. "Fine. I'm a thirty-two-year-old Kate Spade purse mogul. I've just met the world's sexiest man at Fashion Week and we're going out on our first date."

"Why the first date and not your wedding day?" she asks, pulling all of her long brown hair over to one shoulder the way so many white girls are genetically engineered to do.

"That's like reading the end of a good book first. What about you? Who are you tonight?"

"A lonely old fart."

I shoot her a look.

"Kia, I live here. They may not know my name, but quite a few of them know my tattoo." She lowers her voice to a whisper and gestures toward her cooch, "I've got a rather memorable one down there."

I laugh so loud half the bar turns to look at me. "Get out!"

"I wish I could chalk it up to youth, but the ink is barely dry."

"Point one out for me, Karin. I want to see your type."

"My type? That's easy. A fat wallet and a great big cock."

That word always makes me cringe. "Just point one out, already."

Without skipping a beat, she gestures over her right bony shoulder. "The tall blond . . ."

I spot him instantly with his ever-so-gelled spiky hair.

"And the Irish bloke wearing glasses he's talking to . . ."

His freshly manicured hand effortlessly holds a champagne glass.

"And the one in the slim-fitting Co-Op shirt with the handsome smile over there in the corner."

I'm somewhat thrown by this. "The black guy?"

"Yes, is that not proper form where you are from?"

"I just didn't think you'd be into it."

It occurs to me that if I find black men to be the sexiest in the world, why shouldn't she?

"I'm thirty-nine, I'm into everything."

That's obvious since she's done half the room. I check out the black guy again. He's a pretty boy and he really does have a handsome smile. A rarity in these parts. The English aren't really into teeth. As in the straightening or whitening of them. But, hey, we lack manners, they lack Crest whitening strips. I've learned to look past it.

"You've got a type all right . . . fay," I tell her.

"It's either that or Neanderthal. At least when you spend the night at a metro's place, you can share their products in the morning."

"I've got sort of the same dilemma at home. I can either date corny or thug. There's nothing in between."

Karin seems thrown by my slang.

"Either the brotha wears his pants too high—nearly to his chest—or too low—hanging off his ass," I explain.

"Gotcha. On the flight over you mentioned something about breaking up with a bloke? Which one is he?"

"Flash? He wears his pants just right. It's just everything else about him is wrong. Wrong for me, at least."

"And what is right for you?"

"I don't know, Karin. I guess I'll know it when I see it."

"That may work when shopping for the perfect dress, but it's hardly good enough when shopping for the perfect man."

Maybe that's the missing component? Maybe the key to happiness lies in knowing exactly what it takes to make you happy? Of course, I haven't a clue . . .

I glance back at Karin's other two lovers. "Did you know they were friends before you slept with both of them?"

"I was dating Jed, the tall one. He had a party at his flat. A

few of us had done some X. Jed remembered a fantasy I told
him about; how I wanted to do it with two guys. We decided on
Charles and he was game."

*Hold the phone. When did I become such a prude? When did
two at a time become the standard?*

"I don't remember much about the night, except that I had
a bloody good time. I broke things off with Jed shortly after-
wards."

"Why?"

"Come on, Kia. I slept with one of his friends. It was just a
matter of time before it bothered him so much that he'd break
up with me. Besides, he saw the size of Charles's cock and my
reaction to it. We both knew an upgrade was in order."

What is it with white girls and the word *cock*? A cock is a
male chicken. It's something you do to a gun. It's not something
you suck, and it's certainly not something you fuck. That's what
dicks are for.

"Anyway, I'm glad to see they were able to remain on good
terms," she says, lighting up a cigarette. "I take it you've never
had a threesome?"

"Funny you should say that. I was offered to partake in one
earlier today."

She leans in particularly close to me. "Do tell."

"Some prepubescent fab couple wanted me to join them for
drinks tonight."

Seeing as I have nothing further to add, Karin scoffs at me.

"So, when I asked you to drinks did you think I wanted to
boff you, too?"

"You had to be there, all right? I know when I'm being
hit on."

"Assuming you're right, you said they were young and fab.
Why dismiss it so quickly?"

"Because . . ."

That's all I got. I sip my newly arrived drink.

"Because of the girl?"

"Well, yeah, because of the girl."

"So you'd consider it if it was two blokes?"

"Karin, I'm having a hard enough time trying to find one guy I want to sleep with . . ."

"Oh, but you did find one, you just blew him off. If you're dreaming about being thirty-two, that means you're probably, like, thirty-five, which means you're just a few birthdays shy of when hotties stop asking to see you naked. With or without a third party involved."

She's got a point there.

Karin continues: "You Americans are such bullies on the playground and pansies in the bedroom. Both extremely unflattering qualities in a grown-up."

"I'm not a pansy, Karin. Threesomes just sound greedy to me."

"Boom or bust, love. Boom or bust."

I decide to shine the spotlight on her for a while. "All right, so what's your deal?"

"My deal is that I didn't become a flight attendant because I flunked out of cosmetology school. I was a funds manager for many years. Made a shitload of money, most of which I blew on partying and clothes. I looked up one day and realized I hated my life and I was this close to becoming a drug head, or worse— Carrie Bradshaw on *Sex and the City*. So I quit my job and took to the skies. I don't make half the money but I'm twice as happy. That is, of course, when I'm not contemplating strangling myself with a pair of pantyhose. The only reason I haven't done it already is that I don't own a pair of pantyhose."

"And in this suicide scenario of yours, what does the note say?"

"I don't think anyone has ever asked me that before." Karin

seems oddly impressed. "I was thinking of going with, 'It's all your fault.' The *you* being a plural, all-inclusive, everyone-I've-ever-met *you*."

"Excellent move. As your attorney, I advise never to admit guilt or accept blame, even for your own suicide."

"You also mentioned in the middle of your hysterics that you were suspended from your job. What happened?"

Geez, I was a little loose with the tongue. The only thing I didn't blurt out was my Social Security number and my mother's maiden name.

"I disregarded a direct order from my boss. An order I thought was cruel and excessive."

"Your boss is a total wanker, is he?"

"You got it. The good news is that my suspension runs con-current with my vacation. So I'm not really out any money—at least in the short run. Certainly future raises may be out of the question."

"Is that the worst of it, Kia? No raises?"

"Downey. Downey is the worst of it."

"Downey?" Karin asks.

"Just like cops, we're assigned to districts and certain types of crimes. Right now I'm in a prime district eight miles from my house, and I prosecute assault and homicide cases."

"And that's a good thing?"

"The more horrible and heinous the crime, the better."

Karin rolls her eyes at me. "As if I didn't think you Ameri-cans were weird before . . ."

"If I don't stop pushing my liberal agenda, as my boss calls it, and agree to play ball, I'll be prosecuting shoplifters in Downey. That's like being sent down to the minors."

Again, Karin has no idea what I'm talking about.

"It's like one day you're the butler for the Queen and the next you're fetching sticks for her dog. So, you see, Karin, I'm the one who should be contemplating suicide, because not only is my love life in the toilet, so is my career."

"Ahh, but you still have your health, love."

"Nobody cares I've had a crystal clear Pap smear for the last five years. Like it or not, three things mark a woman's progression in life: her marriage, the birth of her children, and lastly, her success at work. I could deal with not having the first two because I was kicking ass on the third. But now . . ."

"But now you're just a three-time loser."

I shoot her a look. "Hey, easy there."

"That is what you're afraid of, that that's what people will think?"

She knows it is, so I don't bother answering. "Can we just get back to our dream lives, Karin?"

"I'm a twenty-five-year-old UNICEF volunteer. Traveling the world helping refugees with my doctor husband who's just patented the cure for AIDS, which, of course, gives us the financial freedom to fly to Milan on the weekends so I can bathe in champagne while patting myself dry with frivolously expensive clothes," Karin says.

"Sort of a Paris Hilton with a heart?"

"It's all about balance, love. None of us thought we'd be here. Late thirties. Single. Glass ceiling cracking our skulls. Mum on our case. But here we are . . ."

"Whoopee," I say, flatly.

"My advice is don't be afraid to shake things up a bit."

"I'm not afraid . . ."

Karin cuts me off. "Bollocks. You were afraid to come on this trip by yourself, and now you're afraid to let loose while on it."

"I passed on a threesome, Karin. Sue me."

"Just promise me something."

"What?" I ask, even though I'm afraid to hear what it is.

"Promise me you'll do one thing in each city that you've

never done before. Something that pushes the envelope a little. And they don't all have to be sexual, but I'll be so delighted to hear about them if they are."

I think on her challenge for a minute. It wouldn't hurt to expand my horizons a bit. It doesn't make sense to have come all this way just to do the same things I do at home.

"Bet," I say with a drunken confidence I hope is there tomorrow.

"What are we betting exactly?"

"*Bet* is slang for *okay*."

As Karin laughs at her mistake, I check out her black friend. His smile seems even brighter than before.

"You know . . . I've never slept with a guy one of my friends has slept with."

Karin follows my eye line across the room. "I'm betting you've never been peed on as an act of foreplay, either."

I look away from him, horrified. "I prefer to be showered with gifts, not urine."

"Me, too. Glad to see you're getting in the spirit of the game, though."

She winks at me and motions to the bartender once more for another round.

Thirteen

Toto, I have a feeling we're not in Kansas anymore.
—*Dorothy, American fictional icon*

THE MILLENNIUM KNIGHTSBRIDGE is a fly boutique hotel located in the heart of chichi London. It's so me.

A tall, burly doorman opens the door for me. "Good evening, ma'am. I believe there are some guests waiting for you at the front desk."

"You must have me confused with someone else. I just left the only person in London I know."

"Are you Kia? Kia from America without a sir name?"

Sir name? What is he talking about? I think for a beat. *Oh—surname! He means last name.*

"It's Carson."

"Nice to meet you, Ms. Carson. Please check with the front desk anyway. I'm pretty sure they're looking for you."

I don't get but two feet inside the door before hearing my name shouted from across the lobby. There in all their ménage-à-trois glory stand Derrick, looking lip-smacking good, and Rita, looking prettier than I remember.

"What are you guys doing here?"

"Trying to leave you a message. We wanted you to meet us at this after-hours spot we found around the corner. But we didn't have your room number or your surname, and Bernard here wasn't coughing up any info," Derrick replies.

Bernard nods his head at me. "It's our policy to protect the privacy of our guests. Especially young ladies traveling unaccompanied."

I smile appreciatively. We all know he did the right thing. Another reason to love this hotel. That and the four-hundred-thread-count linens.

"It's so sweet of you guys to think about me, but I'm a little tipsy and I should probably just go to bed."

"But we brought you a party favor." Rita motions to a man sitting in one of the lobby's many comfortable chairs to come join us.

He gives me a firm handshake as well as a kiss, kiss. "I'm Angelou."

By his accent, I'd say he was Nigerian. By his gear, I'd say he was a nerd. On closer inspection, though, I see that he's built like an American football player. A lean, mean, football player. Hmmm, I didn't see this little plot twist coming.

"One drink," I say.

Rita takes my arm in hers. "Brilliant!"

"So it appears you do know a few Brits, after all," the doorman says as we walk out of the hotel.

"Good looking out," I reply, unsure if my slang translates.

His nod and smile tell me that it does.

Two hours and too many drinks later, Rita, Derrick, and I are working it out on the dance floor like it's the last party of our lives. I've grown quite accustomed to sharing a dance partner. Whether it's with Maya and her boyfriend, Aaron, or with Diane and Leo, I'm always Third-wheel Teri. Why should being eight thousand miles away from home change that?

Angelou turned out to be a bust. He didn't want to dance. Didn't really want to talk, except about his recent breakup with his Swedish girlfriend. According to Rita it's the recent trend here. It's not just black men dating white women anymore. It's black, black men dating white, white women. Rita had hoped she could bring Angelou back into the fold by introducing him to me, but nothing doing. Times are hard when even African men ain't feeling us sistas.

"I'm going to the loo," Derrick announces, leaving Rita and me to bounce to the beat alone.

The DJ is playing everything from Usher to James Brown, "Stayin' Alive" to "Baby Boy." Rita and I are having a friendly little dance-off; she grinds her hips, I shake my ass. She gives a little Beyoncé. I throw her a little Janet. It's hot. It's sexy. It's R. Kelly. The DJ is remixing the remix of "Step in the Name of Love." Rita and I begin to do a cha-cha/stepping combo dance. It's a little awkward, neither of us knowing who should lead. Feeling myself, I decide to take charge.

I sing along to the music. "Let me see you do the l-o-v-e s-l-i-d-e."

And on the *s-l-i-d-e*, she kissed me. For real. With tongue and everything. Awkward to the nth degree. Junior high quality at best. Let's be clear, I give good head, but I'm a great kisser. At least I thought so. No matter how this turns out, I'm going to need therapy for sure. I try to shut my mind off and just go with it. No, no, that's not working. All I keep thinking is, *Am I doing this right?* I keep my eyes closed for fear that her expression will prove that I'm not. Kissing a woman should be the same as kissing a guy, right? Same body parts involved. There's no innie-where-there-should-be-an-outie issue to deal with. But, no, kissing a woman is completely different than kissing a man. I'd never really given it much thought before, but with a man you're bound to have a lip or a cheek brush up against some degree of facial hair, sometimes with disastrous results. There's nothing sexy about having your face cut up by prickly razor stubble. But her skin is so smooth. I can see why men like kissing us; it's like sleeping on satin sheets. But for some reason, despite what should be seen as a plus, I'm not liking it at all.

"I can't believe you two started the party without me," I hear Derrick say.

And before I know it, Derrick and I are kissing. Oh yeah, it's all coming back to me now. Rita had me up here thinking I'd forgotten how to kiss. I know how to kiss. And, God forgive me, so does her man.

"Uh, hello?" Rita says.

I pull away from Derrick to see Rita standing there like she's the last kid picked for the kickball team. I'm at a total loss here. What's the protocol for a situation like this? I look down at my red Stuart Weitzman three-inch espadrilles. Click, click, click. Shit! Clicking her heels may have worked for Dorothy, but my ass is still here.

"I'm down for whatever, you know, but I thought it was supposed to be the three of us?" Rita says, her voice screeching up an octave with each word.

"But it was fine when you two were going at it?" Derrick asks.

"That just sort of happened," Rita explains.

While they argue back and forth it dawns on me I wasn't going to need therapy, because I was clear about one thing: I'm not a threesome kind of girl. It's not only greedy, it's messy.

"Thanks for showing me a great time and everything, but I think I'm going to call it a night."

I grab my purse from a nearby couch where Angelou sits in a catatonic sulk. I wave goodbye to him before giving Rita a kiss, kiss. On the cheek, of course. I start to do the same to Derrick, but think better of it and shake his hand instead.

For the second time today, I find myself fleeing the scene. This time, however, I don't look back.

Fourteen

The earth belongs to anyone who stops for a moment, gazes and goes on his way...
—*Colette, French author*

I'M STRUGGLING TO OPEN MY EYES. It's a losing battle for the longest time. But since my hotel phone won't stop ringing, I force them open, willing myself to win the war in order to quiet the room.

"Hello." My drag-queen voice is back.

"Dang, Kia, you sound awful."

"Matches how I feel."

"So much for wishing you top of the morning."

"That's Irish, Diane."

"Whatever. They're both white and bow to the same queen."

I glance at the clock. It's nine A.M. in England. Midnight in L.A.

"What are you doing up? I thought women in your condition ate and slept their way through pregnancy?"

"I took a nap earlier. Now I can't sleep."

"Well, Di, I was sleeping just fine, thank you."

"Wake up and talk to me. I miss you," she whines.

I try to sit up, but it's not going over so well. "I miss you, too. How's the little it doing?"

"Making me sick 24/7. I gag all day long and my mouth feels

like I've been sucking on a penny. Mom said the first trimester was the worst for her, too."

"Hold on, Di. All this talk of puking has made me want to." I grab a Perrier out of the mini-bar. I could feed a kid in Somalia for a year on what this damn thing is going to cost me.

"Hangover, huh? I want to hear all the details."

The only details she'd be interested in are the ones I'm not sure I want to tell.

"How's Mom?" I ask.

"How do you think? Monitoring everything I eat, how many hours I work. She's driving me up a wall already and the baby's not due until March."

"You know she means well."

"It's the only reason she's still breathing. Unfortunately it's down my neck."

I eke out a small laugh.

"I guess you're feeling better?"

"A thirty-dollar snack will do that to you," I reply.

I've opened up a package of crackers as well. They seem to be helping.

"London's cool, but it's hard on the purse."

"Geez, Kia, you've been there a week and that's all you got? That the place is expensive?"

That is kind of wack. If I don't give her something she's going to think I'm not having a good time. She'll feel guilty, and I don't want that. Her pregnancy was the best thing to happen to us both. I needed to take this trip and I needed to take it alone. You find out a lot about yourself when you're by yourself.

"Didn't you tell me once you regretted not having an affair with a woman before you got married?"

Diane laughs. "Yeah, I can see me saying something crazy like that."

"Well, get over it. It ain't all that. They may have soft skin, but their mouths are too damn small."

"What are you saying, Kia?"

"I never really thought about it before but men have big mouths. When you kiss them it's like exploring the Grand Canyon. Kissing a woman is like exploring a rabbit hole. The story is over before it even gets started."

There is silence on the phone.

"Hello? Di?"

"I'm here. I'm freaked out, but I'm here. Was she pretty?"

"Of course."

"Was she black?"

"Of course."

"Were you drunk?"

"Of course."

"Kia, I don't think it counts if you're drunk."

"I think her man would disagree with you on that, Di."

"Quit playing. I'm supposed to believe you kissed a babe while her man watched?"

"No."

"Yeah, that's what I thought," she says smugly.

"A babe kissed me while her man watched. Then her man kissed me while the babe watched."

"Kia, you're lying!"

"No, I'm not."

"And then what happened?"

"I realized I wasn't gay or bi. And that all of Mom's spankings were in vain, because I still don't like to share."

Diane laughs hysterically. "I can't believe you went on this trip without me and have the nerve to have a good time!"

"Would it help if I said you are sorely missed?"

"Just come home soon, okay? Squeezing Leo's hand at Sunday dinner isn't quite the same. He squeals like a girl."

The thought of my family all gathered around the table has me feeling a bit homesick. As much as Di and I gripe about it, only something as big as the Atlantic Ocean could keep either of us from being there.

"I love you, Di. Give everyone a big kiss for me."

"Love you, too. Hey, Kia?"

"Yeah?"

"If you're kissing girls in London, I can't wait to see what you'll do in Paris."

"Me neither."

Fifteen

> . . . Paris is a moveable feast.
> —*Ernest Hemingway, American author*

THERE'S A SAYING we Americans like to cloak ourselves in: *Only in America* . . .

Only in America could an Austrian bodybuilder become the head of the eighth most powerful nation in the world, otherwise known as the state of California. Only in America could a poor black girl from the country grow up to become a billion-dollar media diva-naire. Only in America can a nobody become a somebody overnight.

But she proved the saying wrong. She being Paris. She being Josephine Baker. Unable to be true to herself in the States, this penniless, bowlegged, honey-colored, squeaky-voiced, topless dancer came to the City of Light and turned the shit out.

Only in Paris could this woman many thought was a man become the most celebrated entertainer of her age. Only in Paris could this nonsmoker play an instrumental part in stopping the Nazis by smuggling microfilm containing a German codebook inside of a hollowed-out cigarette. Only in Paris did twenty thousand people line the streets, the same streets I'm walking on now, for a glimpse of her coffin as it passed by. Policemen saluted. Men removed their hats. Women waved handkerchiefs.

Only in Paris.

How sad is it that she had to travel so far to fulfill her divine potential? A small part of me wonders if that is to be my fate as well? How long can I keep tap dancing for massa and still be able to look at myself in the mirror? What if I've picked the wrong life for myself? Maybe I should've gone to design school. Maybe I should've gone to design school in Paris.

And so I've spent the day wandering the streets of Montmartre in search of the Paris Josephine Baker and countless other black Americans called home when Lady Liberty had reneged on all of her promises.

"Excusez-moi. Parlez-vous anglais?" I ask a police officer with the aid of my English-to-French phrase book.

"A little," he says.

"Can you please tell me how to get to Rue Pigalle?"

"Pigalle? You sure is place you want go, mademoiselle?"

"Yes," I say. The street may not hold any significance for him, a white Frenchman, but to me, a black American, it's the 125th Street in Harlem of France. It's where expats like Eugene Bullard, the first black combat pilot, opened businesses. It's where James Baldwin wrote *Go Tell It on the Mountain*.

Having followed the policeman's directions to a T, I find myself standing amongst a group of rather nondescript, completely unimpressive buildings. Where are the sexy cafés and nightclubs? The jazz sonnets I expected to hear at every turn? More to the point, where are the black people—the storeowners, artists, and musicians I had imagined would be here welcoming me with open arms?

It doesn't take long before my Robert Clergerie patent-leather sandals begin to give me blisters. The pragmatist in me really wanted to wear sensible shoes today, but it turns out I didn't pack any. At least none that looked cute with my pink linen sundress.

Since all of the buildings lack signage, I decide to enter one at random. Tired, thirsty, and frustrated, I'm no longer in search of Harlem, past or present, just a place to rest my aching dogs, and maybe get a drink.

It takes a moment for my eyes to adjust to the dark, moody lighting. But once they do, I'm pleased to see that I have found a place to accomplish both my goals. I sit at a table near the door and order a glass of the house wine. The waiter shoots me a strange look, but I'm too pooped to try and decipher its meaning. My eyes are drawn to a stage decorated to look like a boudoir. A circular bed rests in the center, dressed in crimson satin sheets with a maroon velvet duvet cover. Very Ralph Lauren Home Collection. Love! I'm obsessed with sheets. High-end sheets. A live jazz quartet begins playing a sexy little tune. I check my watch. It's six P.M., barely dark outside. I must have stumbled across a dinner-theater venue. Hey, it's not the Chitlin' Circuit, but it could be cute.

Suddenly, a woman descends from the ceiling on a trapeze, à la Nicole Kidman in *Moulin Rouge*. The woman appears to be . . . well, she appears to be a dwarf. A dwarf in a white La Perla, baby-doll negligee. Love! The negligee, that is.

Seeing a little person, as I now remember they like to be called, dancing around in her underwear takes more than a minute to get used to, but when she begins belting out a tune like she's Ella Fitzgerald, I forget about her stature and focus only on her voice. It seems I've stumbled across a burlesque dinner theater. Love! And I'm not the only one, since this place is about sixty-percent occupied. Maybe thirty people or so. Mostly couples, no big surprise there.

A baritone voice begins accompanying her, but I can't locate where it's coming from. Just then a hole in the stage floor opens up and out emerges a six-foot-six, two-hundred-and-fifty-pound specimen of a man. A black man. Love! The two sing an amazing duet—in French, of course. Marveling at the theatrics of it all, I look inside my purse for my camera. I glance back toward the stage just in time to catch the six-foot-six chocolate thunder of a man tossing the three-foot-three white cloud of a woman face down onto the red sun of a bed. He begins doing something that, well . . . let's just say it's illegal in thirty-nine states. I snap a quick photo—Lorna did ask that I take plenty of pictures—and flee the freak show, thinking only one thing: Only in Paris . . .

The Algerian, English-speaking cab driver who is now taking me back to my hotel informs me that Pigalle was teeming with black artisans in the years between the two world wars, but Germany's occupation of Paris caused most of the black Americans living there to return to the States. Hitler trumps Jim Crow any day of the week. Many came back again in the fifties, but by then Pigalle had become the official red-light district of Paris. *C'est la vie*, 125th Street of France.

As we roll by the Champs-Élysées, the Arc de Triomphe in the distance, I realize that Paris is everything a woman and a city should be. Engaging. Elegant. Sensual. Hard to love. Harder to leave. She's also everything most women and big cities really are. Seedy. Spiteful. Two-faced. Dying to be loved. Dying to be left the hell alone. In the end, all you can do is surrender to her charms and bad moods and pray that the love you feel for her outweighs your desire to strangle her as she sleeps.

Being in Paris is like, I imagine, being on ecstasy. Colors are more vivid. Your hearing more acute. Your imagination more expansive. You want to touch and feel everything. Which can be bad, if your desire is to reach out and touch fire. Earlier today, while at the Café de la Paix, I caught myself sketching a design for a purse on a napkin. A purse I actually had visions of going home and making. I haven't made anything since college, when somehow I got it in my head that I had to put aside the creative part of myself in order to be taken seriously. It's sort of the pretty-girl curse. Not that pretty girls have it hard, because, compared to the alternative, we don't; but when God put a viable working brain inside a pretty girl's head, he created a monster of a dilemma. America is a very label-driven society. And while its citizens are allowed to add new labels to their résumé, it's really more of an exchange program. In order to add a new label, you must turn in an old one. Arnold Schwarzenegger can't be the governor of California *and* the current Mr. Olympiad. A person can't be both public-service-oriented *and* incredibly vain at the same time. Right? But in Paris, contradictions thrive. You can be pretty and smart. Black and beautiful. In Paris it is possible to witness the Cirque du Soleil do porn. In Paris it's possible to both lose and find yourself at the same time. And that's when I got it. Paris is an experience, more than anything else. Sure, there are plenty of sanctioned sights to see— Versailles, Notre Dame—but that's not why *they* came. Musicians like Louis Armstrong and Mahalia Jackson. Writers like Langston Hughes and Richard Wright. Scholars like Paul Robeson and W.E.B. Du Bois.

They came for the food. The five-and-a-half-hour six-course meals. The three hundred and sixty-two different kinds of cheese.

They came for the fashion. The way women garden in scarves and high heels, reserving tennis shoes for the times they actually play tennis.

They came for the freedom. The freedom to create. The freedom to express themselves. The freedom to be accepted and respected in every way denied to them back home.

Don't get it twisted; the French can be racist as anybody else. My cab driver explained that the Algerians, who get it from all sides, being both African and Muslim, are the objects of scorn here. But for whatever reason, the French love black Americans. I'm betting it's just to piss off white Americans, but I'll take love wherever I can get it. Even if it is . . . only in Paris.

Sixteen

Wouldn't take nothing for my journey now.
—*Maya Angelou, African-American author*

IF A GIRL HAS TO TURN thirty-five, then this is the way to do it: check into a quaint hotel overlooking the Seine, the river that divides Paris in half. Have breakfast in bed—Belgian waffles with fresh strawberries, a juicy slice of ham, scrambled eggs with brie and onions, a steaming cup of hot cocoa (the French love the stuff), and as many mimosas as one can down. Oh, and open presents.

Maya gave me a journal only a real broad would dare to carry: a five-by-eight, fire-engine-red, Italian-leather-bound journal. I was a bit disappointed to see she didn't enclose a card. Maya's that girl. That *always enclose a card with a special thought, handwritten in nouveau calligraphy* type girl. Maya not including a card is like Kobe without Shaq. Cute but where's the muscle?

I run my hands across the baby-soft pristine cover and wonder how long will it take before I spill something on it? A journal. A sweet and thoughtful gesture, albeit thoroughly anxiety-inducing. A journal such as this deserves profound thoughts. Witty musings. Soul-baring confessions. I'm not up to the task. I mean, I crack a few jokes every now and again, but nothing funny enough to be preserved for all posterity. I remember having profound thoughts in college, but certainly none since. And, according to Karin, I have nothing to confess, as I apparently haven't done squat.

I could write about going to the Louvre, once a palace for kings, now the world's largest and most famous museum. How cultured and intellectual the outing made me feel. How seeing the *Mona Lisa* brought hope into my life. If a wallflower like her can marry a Florentine millionaire and become immortalized in one of the most famous paintings of all time, surely I can, at the very least, expect to get laid again. But I can't write that. The truth is, the Louvre was a little underwhelming. How long do I have to gaze at portraits of dainty white maidens whose only idea of suffering is having to wear the baby-blue gown instead of the pink one to the ball before being allowed to shop completely guilt free? Forty-eight and a half minutes, it turns out.

I flip through the book's pages. A smile creeps across my face. Shaq has just entered the building. Maya has indeed written me a note.

Yes, girl, the first page of your journal will be written by me. Not because I'm an egomaniac, although I have my moments, but because I want the record to show what an amazing person you are. I'm afraid you'll overlook that in your memoirs. Journals tend to be a place we seek comfort in when our lives are falling apart. When you've just found out that you didn't get the job you really didn't want but funds were getting tight so you considered it, and now you're pissed that you did because it turns out you weren't right for it anyway. Wait, that's my life not yours . . . The point is, in our low moments we tend to think it's our fault. We blame ourselves and go in search of something to fix. If I were skinnier he wouldn't have left. If I were smarter they wouldn't have fired me. If I were white . . . why even open Pandora's box with that one, the world being their oyster and all.

I just want the record to show that there's nothing to fix. You're a great lawyer, a great friend, and a really great woman. And damn all those who don't get it!

Love, Maya

She's that girl, all right.

How did she know? How did she know that was exactly what I needed to hear? I haven't mentioned word one about my suspension to Maya or anyone back home, so either my best friend has ESP or, as I'm coming to realize, she was projecting. This letter was written for her sake as much as my own. Being unemployed has been hard on her. We've all been taught that a man's identity is tied to his job, but no one prepares a woman for that reality. As black women we have to prove ourselves over and over again. Prove to everyone that we weren't just hired to fill a *twofer* quota. We spend a majority of our day either working at our job or worrying about it. And when it's gone, you can't help but feel a little out of sorts. It's no wonder we all need a pep talk now and again. When we're going through the negative evolutions of life, there's nothing like a little sisterhood rah-rah from a Maya, Shaniqua, Maria, Tiffany, or even ourselves to help get us through.

I struggle to get out of bed without spilling my breakfast over, as there is a knock at my door. I open it to find a bellman holding an exquisite bouquet of long-stem white lilies. I'm floored. It's so unexpected yet so perfect for the moment I'm having.

"May I bring them in, mademoiselle?"

"Yes, please," I say, ushering him inside and then quickly ushering him out.

I know I should tip him but I'm in no mood to calculate euros into dollars right now. I'll get it wrong and I'll either insult the bastard by giving him sixty-three cents or I'll kick myself because the SOB is now walking around with bail money. No thank you. I'm enjoying myself way too much for that head trip.

I glance at the towering white forest in front of me. Flash. They've got to be from Flash. Wow. You hang up on a man and he sends you flowers. What would happen if I really decided to treat him like shit? He'd probably fall hopelessly in love. Bastard. I tear open the envelope.

Sorry about the suspension. Oh yeah, Happy Fortieth!
Drew.

Drew? DREW? Barb must have told him where I was staying. She sent me a nice fruit basket with a note.

The journey, not the arrival matters (unless you're the travel
agent). I trust you arrived in good spirits.
Happy Birthday and Godspeed, Barb.

Genius customer-service ploy, I'll give her that.

Forty. Drew knows good and well I'm only a year older than him. I'll bet my suspension is the talk of the office. I'm so glad I'm not there to hear any of it. Screw work. And screw Drew for making me think about work.

I stare at the flowers. They're breathtaking, really. Just the right amount of greens, the lilies opened just a hairsbreadth shy of their full bloom. No one has ever sent me lilies before. Guess I have to call and thank him. It's two A.M. there. Perfect. I can just text-message his cell. I'll have fulfilled my Miss Manners obligation without any personal contact.

Thx 4 lilies. I got your f-ing 40. C U when I get back.
Kia.

I push send. *And Maya thinks I can fill a journal. I can't even fill a cell phone.* I pour myself another mimosa, minus the OJ. Who needs the extra calories? I'm sure my old bones could use the calcium, but the French probably don't add calcium to their freshly squeezed orange juice, anyway. These are the kinds of profound thoughts I have nowadays. The hotel phone rings and I jump up to answer it.

"*Bonjour,*" I say as if raised by Coco Chanel.

"*Bonjour, mademoiselle. J'espère les français êtes vous bien.*"

I repeat back my recent mantra. "*Excusez-moi. No parler français.*"

"Good, because '*I hope the French are treating you well*' is about all the French I know and I doubt I even got that right."

Damn, if I wanted to talk to his ass I would've called him.

"Drew, what are you doing up?"

"Packing. I leave tomorrow for Morocco."

"Morocco? What's in Morocco?"

"I don't know, Carson. Moroccans. Great food, really cool art . . ."

"All right, it was a dumb question. There's a whole world out there and it deserves to be seen."

"Don't tell me Europe has gotten to you? I wasn't sure if you were going to like it. It *is* full of Europeans, after all."

"Ha, ha. So far the people have been real decent. Don't get me wrong, the place could certainly use more brothas roaming around, and I mean from Atlanta and not Africa, 'cause that's just a whole different flavor all together . . ."

"What's with the bullshit text message? I wasn't expecting a blow job, but a personal thank-you would've been nice."

"Drew, I thought you'd be asleep. I was being polite."

"You were being a chickenshit."

I hate that he knows me so well. Of course I was being a chickenshit.

"I just didn't want to have a big work conversation. Getting suspended is the most embarrassing thing that's ever happened to me. It's something I'd rather not think about right now. I'm on vacation. Happy thoughts only."

"But you have nothing to be embarrassed about, Carson. You did the right thing by that kid. You usually do. It's just one of your many annoying qualities."

Both he and my mother share the same backhanded-compliment gene, I see.

"Yeah, well, what are my others?"

"The way you're always so pulled together. Your-purse-matches-your-shoes kind of stuff. Everybody has an off day, but not you."

Who knew he paid attention to such things?

"Hey, that's all Lorna's doing."

That wasn't entirely true. Mom did always tell us to look our best, but I wasn't going to tell him I lived in constant fear that the one time I'm not pulled together is when I'm going to run into my Prince Charming. And he'll look right past me because, well, my purse doesn't match my shoes.

I can't tell him that I make an extra effort to look nice on the off chance that I run into a married girlfriend and when they ask if I'm married, and they always ask, and I always have to shake my head no, at least they don't walk away thinking it's totally my fault because I've let myself go. I can't tell him that as a black woman working within the confines of a white male establishment, I sometimes resort to using my feminine wiles to get a judge to rule in my favor. Everybody knows a smart, uppity negra gets overruled. A smartly dressed one gets sustained . . . at least some of the time.

It's hard work looking so effortlessly fabulous. It's not a quality. It's a curse. But I can't say any of that.

"Thanks for the flowers. And, you know, for remembering my birthday."

"You'd do the same for me."

"No, Drew, I don't think I would."

"Last year when I was sick as a dog on my birthday, who had chicken noodle soup from Canter's Deli, Popsicles, and a quart of orange juice delivered to my house? And let's not forget the videos from Blockbuster and the *Playboy* magazine. First class all they way, Carson."

How could I have forgotten about that? With the delivery charge, that must have set me back a hundred bucks easily. What kind of crack was I smoking that day?

"Hey, if you go topless in Mykonos, take a picture for me."

"Sure, Drew. And when you grow a set of balls, you do the same."

Drew lets out an easy laugh.

"Listen, you've wasted enough money on me. Have a really great trip. I'll see you back in L.A.," I say.

"Not if I see you first."

I hang up feeling bad I didn't tell him that sending flowers to Paris was first class all the way, too. I catch myself frowning. I should definitely schedule a facial for later. A married woman can sport forehead wrinkles, a single one with limited savings and a lukewarm career cannot.

Pouring myself more bubbly, I declare this to be a champagne-only day. I don't know what it is, champagne just tastes better in Paris.

Seventeen

People travel to faraway places to watch in fascina-
tion the kind of people they ignore at home.
—*Dagobert D. Runes, American author*

"BONJOUR," I say to the salesgirl upon entering my ump-
teenth boutique.

"*Bonjour*," she offers back.

On my first shopping trip, a whopping three hours after
landing at de Gaulle Airport, I would enter a store and wait for
the salesgirl to speak to me. When she didn't, I'd storm out,
vowing not to shop where my black dollars weren't appreci-
ated. Each time it happened I grew more frustrated, yet was de-
termined not to give in.

But then I saw the shirt. The shirt I had to have, but had no
business buying under such hostile circumstances. I stared at
the darn thing for thirty minutes, envisioning all the places I
could wear such a splendid creation: a salmon-colored halter
number.

Woman after woman entered the tiny shop. *Bonjour*, they'd
say. And without fail, a polite *Bonjour* would be returned. And
then it dawned on me: the customers spoke first.

"*Bonjour*," I said meekly.

"*Bonjour*," I heard back in a sweet, welcoming voice.

Holy shit, it's not a black thing. It's a French thing. The cus-
tomer speaks first. It goes without saying I bought the blouse. It

matches perfectly with my brown silk skirt, my coral Calvin Klein mules, and the vintage Louis Vuitton tootsie-roll purse I've chosen to wear on today's shopping adventure. Catching my reflection in a store mirror, I have to admit, Drew is right— I *do* know how to pull a look together.

A light citrus scent trickles through the air, causing me to greedily fill my lungs. And then I hear a voice. It sounds like . . . wisdom. Deep and purposeful.

"*Bonjour*," the woman says to the salesgirl, obviously not giving a hoot whether she responds in kind.

I can tell by the way the shopgirl throws the woman a lingering smile she senses it, too. There's just something about her. Maybe it's her eyes? No, they're nothing special, just a soft brown. Looking at her, I see she's not a classic French beauty, like Catherine Denevue or even Juliet Binoche. Her face is more handsome than pretty, and I'm betting she figured that out early on and has made an extra effort to find other ways to stand out in a crowd. Her tall, lean physique certainly helps. She towers over the petite salesgirl, who hasn't left her side since she walked through the door. She's not WNBA-tall, just long-blades-of-grass tall. Long blades of grass in heels. Christian Louboutin heels.

It doesn't take her long to pick out quite a few things to try on. A cashmere tank, pink. Three pairs of jeans, all dark denim. A slinky dress, black. Oh my God! I think she's caught me staring at her. I avoid her gaze and fumble through a long rack of pants, quickly selecting a gray pair.

She heads into the dressing room. I grab a few more items— a little black dress, a T-shirt with *Paris* written in red faux gemstones, another little black dress—and head to the dressing room as well.

I must pass by Marie (so I've heard the salesgirl call her) six times as we go in and out of our mirrorless dressing rooms. She smiles approvingly at my choices. Damn straight. Paris may be the world's fashion capital, but that doesn't mean they have a monopoly on good taste.

I wonder how old she is? With white women it's so hard tell. They simply age less gracefully. A fair trade-off since they can go swimming without giving a second thought to getting their hair wet. Taking Marie's smile lines into account, and my lack of them, I'm guessing we're about the same age.

She wins in the posture department, though. She, like a lot of *Parisiennes* I've noticed, stands so naturally erect. Almost as if their spines were fortified with steel. I only do that when I'm performing in court. I'm not a total idiot. They've actually done studies on this stuff: lawyers who slouch, lose.

What does she do for a living, I wonder? If she were a New Yorker, I'd say she was a Broadway actress or a socialite. In L.A., I'd put money on her being the wife of an actor, or a former high-powered studio exec who now has her own independent production company. Who else gets to shop so leisurely in the middle of the day at an expensive boutique?

I'm kicking myself for studying Spanish instead of French in high school and college. I'm dying to know what she and the salesgirl are gabbing about.

Everything Marie selects to try on suits her perfectly. Just the right size, the right colors for her skin tone. Maybe that's what it is about her—she just knows herself.

I've found a few things I like, but I have to be careful. I bought eleven pounds of clothes in London. In weight, that is. I shudder to think how many pounds, or rather dollars, I've charged up. I've got three more pounds to go before I'll have to shell out extra cash every time I fly. Aw, screw it. I didn't come this far to let a few bucks stand between me and the most darling little *noir* dress, must-have *bleu* silk slacks, and the same *rose* cashmere tank Miss Thing tried on. It looked great on both of us.

I head to the register, or *caisse* as they call it. I've taken it upon myself to learn a few important French words out of my *Frommer's Fast 'n Easy Phrase Book*. Mostly those dealing with clothes and food. I learned the hard way that ordering a martini here will get you a glass of fortified wine. *Martini americain* will get you the gin-and-vermouth variety. I haven't quite figured out how to order a cosmo, but I'm working on it.

Two hundred and ninety-eight euros later, I head for the door. The euro, the currency used throughout most of Europe, is friendlier than the British pound, but still a bitter pill to swallow for us Yanks. After service fees, three hundred hard-earned American dollars will yield only two hundred and twenty-five euros. The American dollar may be cruising Easy Street in Canada and Australia, but over here it's falling on pretty tough times.

After exiting the shop, I realize I've left behind my sunglasses. As I head for the dressing room, I pass Marie who now stands at the *caisse*. Perfect, now I can see what she has decided to buy.

Someone is using the dressing room I just exited. Someone who does not speak English. I spastically act out to a salesgirl my predicament. It takes her a minute but she finally gets it. She speaks to the woman on my behalf. I can hear the woman unzipping her purse. That French heifer was going to steal my Guccis! *No parler anglais*, my ass. She knew exactly what I was saying. Gucci needs no translation.

"Merci," I say to the salesgirl.

I head back into the main part of the shop in time to see Marie walking out the door with only a tiny bag. A bag too small to fit any of things I saw her try on. I struggle to ask the cashier what Marie purchased. I have no clue how to act it out, so after a few frustratingly inane attempts, I leave the shop, annoyed that I'm annoyed that I don't know what a woman whom I don't even know just bought.

Outside I spot Marie trying to flag a taxi. It becomes clear to me that not knowing what's inside her bag will plague me all day. What kind of woman spends all that time trying on amazing clothes and walks out with so little to show for it? That's just not how it's done.

Just as I decide to ask her, or make a vain attempt to, anyway, she jumps into a taxi.

"Shit!" I mutter to myself as I watch Marie and her little bag drive away.

Another taxi comes to a stop in front of me. My initial reaction is to wave him on, but since I've already shot my shopping wad, I should probably go back to the hotel and wait for my six-o'clock facial. Three long hours from now.

"*Hôtel du Louvre, s'il vous plaît,*" I say to the driver.

"*Oui, mademoiselle.*"

We drive in silence, both of us knowing I've pretty much shot my speaking-French wad as well. We haven't gone too far before I spot Marie getting out of her taxi in front of La Grande Armée, a renowned brasserie that just so happens to be on my must see/do list. Suddenly I'm starving.

"Stop."

He shoots me a confused look. My hotel is a few miles from here.

"Stop!" I say louder.

I know these people understand more than they let on. As if knowing that I know that, he does as he's told. I toss him five euros in change and bolt out of the taxi.

La Grande Armée is owned by two brothers and is designed

to look somewhat like a bordello. Picture black lacquered tables, leopard upholstery, Bordeaux velvet. Whether I catch up to Marie or not, this was a good call.

Within a few minutes I spot the bag and Marie, sitting with a man I presume is her lover. I laugh at myself. Back home I would've said boyfriend, but here I feel the need to use the word *amoureux*.

I score a lucky table in the corner that allows me to watch her somewhat on the sly. I'm starting to feel a little weird about spying on her. Maybe I should just go up to her, pretend our running into each other again is a coincidence, and casually ask what she bought. Or . . . I could get my grub on first and step to her on my way out. I vote for number *deux*.

Luckily I brought along my journal. It'll give me something to do, or pretend to do, as I impersonate a private eye.

I read what I wrote this morning. "*On doit profiter.*" I suppose if I'd found myself celebrating my birthday in Rome I would've written "*Carpe diem.*" The Romans seize the day. The French want to profit from it. They excel at enjoying and living in the moment, believing one should profit from all of life's bounty: a good meal, time shared with friends, and, of course, being in love. I want to live my life like that. Squeezing the most out of every moment.

Over the next two hours I watch Marie as she rests her hand sweetly on her lover's forearm. Twice I catch him running his hand along her jawbone. He plays the comedian, as I hear her throaty giggle too many times to count. She plays the nymph, leaning in to subtly stroke his dick through his jeans. Then she discreetly leads his hand up her thigh, in what appears to be a brief encounter with her crotch. Great, I'm not only a stalker, I'm a Peeping Tom, too.

Under-the-table antics aside, her above-the-table manners

are on point. Marie's silverware never clangs awkwardly against her plate. She takes only appropriately sized bites of her meal. Never dropping even the smallest morsel on the table-cloth or in her lap.

The Europeans eat with the hump of the fork facing toward them; we eat with the hump facing the plate. I've yet to really get the hang of it but I find it does limit the amount of food you can shovel into your mouth—something I often do. Many of my meals happen on the run or not at all. Last I checked, a bag of microwave popcorn didn't qualify as dinner.

The French are wrong about the ice-cube thing. They pre-fer their drinks served at room temperature. Probably because their teeth, like the Brits, are jacked up, too. Drinking a frosty-cold Coca-Cola might cause shooting pain in their mouths like in those Anbesol commercials.

The French are definitely wrong about escargot and truffles. They can call it a delicacy if they want to, but eating snails and fungi is just plain wrong. I'm sure they feel the same about chit-terlings. They'd be wrong about that, too.

But this long lunch, even longer dinner thing, is the truth. I can just imagine how much I would look forward to going to trial if every day at noon, court shut down and we all headed to a local café to eat and drink for three hours. Taxpayers would save millions, as lawyers would scramble to settle cases over a good merlot instead of fighting it out in drab, dreary court-rooms.

One lobster salad and two kir royales (me), half a duck and a whole bottle of wine (her) later, her lover pays the bill. I quickly do the same. I'm not but two feet from the table when my waiter stops me. He motions as if he's writing a check.

"L'addition! L'addition!"

Is he trying to say I've skipped out on the bill? Like I'm some high schooler doing a dine-and-dash at Denny's?

"It's on the table." I'm too frazzled to figure out how to say it in French.

He shakes his head emphatically. *"Non, mademoiselle. Non."*

I spot Marie's lover walking out the door. I rush back to the table, the waiter on my heels.

"Sir, it's right here on the table," I say with righteous indignation.

Only problem is, it isn't. The bill is nowhere to be found. I quickly look under the table. Nothing. A few of the restaurant patrons are starting to take notice of me and my predicament. Some seem sympathetic. Some throw me a *stupid American* scowl the French are often so quick to dispense. I retrace my steps in my head. I remember signing the stupid thing. I remember putting the duplicate copy in my . . . shit! I check my purse and, sure enough, there are both copies of the bill.

I offer him a sweet apologetic smile. "My bad."

I'm mortified. It's an honest mistake but one they'll probably hold against the next one hundred black people who roll through here. The only mea culpa I can offer is to hand the waiter the original receipt and a few extra euros.

"I'm sorry," I say sincerely, all the while making my way to the front door.

To my amazement I discover that Marie's lover has left, but she remains. Casual as can be, sipping coffee as if it were the most pressing thing she had to do in her lifetime.

It's now or never, Kia, I say, trying to psych myself up. I do a little fighter neck roll. I take a deep breath. And I go in.

"Excusez-moi. Parlez-vous anglais?"

"I was wondering if you were going to say something to me," she says.

I'm more embarrassed than ever. "You knew I was watching you?"

"Wasn't positive of it till this very moment."

She got me. As a lawyer, I know the cardinal rule is to always deny, deny, deny.

Marie gently kicks a chair toward me with one of her long legs. "Join me while I finish my coffee. It's simply too good to rush through. Would you care for one?"

"No thank you. I can't put another thing in mouth."

"I hope that malady doesn't last too long. Paris just isn't Paris unless you're stuffing something into your mouth. Food, sometimes a foot, or other more interesting body parts."

As if I wasn't already taken with her, now I find out she's funny, too.

"Where did you learn to speak English so well?" I ask.

"I majored in language studies at the Sorbonne."

It's been a long time since I've been intimidated by another woman, Judge Peete being the last. She probably was fluent in more than one language, too, but she has the face of a pug.

"I'm Kia, by the way."

"Marie."

Hearing her confirm that her name is in fact Marie, gives me a mini thrill.

"What was the Sorbonne like?" I ask eagerly.

"Like any other school, I guess. You didn't attend university?

"Of course. Just not one as prestigious as the Sorbonne."

"You strike me as the sort who went to Yale."

"Please, Marie, don't say that. Every Yalie I know is weird."

"I suppose an American would think spying is perfectly normal behavior."

"But it's not like I was stalking you. I was stalking your bag. I saw you shopping earlier and curiosity got the better of me. I'm dying to know what you bought. I'm loaded down with packages, and you walked away with a bag too small to hold a sneeze."

"You Americans are certainly ones for excess."

"And the French obsession with cheese isn't excessive? The stuff is great on a burger. It's perfect on macaroni. But does one really need to down a plate of it after gorging on a huge meal?"

Marie studies me for a beat. "Aren't you a feisty one."

"I'm certainly more of a fighter than a lover. At least these days, anyway."

"Me, too."

I look at her like she's crazy. "I'm sure your lover would beg to differ."

A concerned look crosses Marie's face. "What do you know about my lover?"

"From what I saw, he seems to be very into you."

"You mean the man I had lunch with? That's my husband. I met my lover for breakfast. You weren't following me then, too, were you?"

Did this heifer just say she has a husband and *a lover? I need to be taking notes.*

"But you and your husband just seemed so in love."

"We are. Americans take lovers when things start to go wrong. We do it so that they never do."

Since I had neither a lover nor a husband, I couldn't possibly argue with such logic.

"Husbands rarely forget your birthday for fear your lover won't. Wives know their husband may not leave them for putting on twenty pounds, but their lover will. Lovers just keep everyone honest."

Again, I'll have to take her word for it. Marie places the bag on the table.

"Kia, did you really follow me here just to find out what's in this bag?"

"I've spent the last few days doing all the things you're supposed to do when you come to Paris—eat, shop, and sight-see.

I've done the Eiffel Tower, the Louvre. But it's my birthday and I didn't want to do anything touristy. And then you walked into the shop. And for the first time I wondered what it would be like to be French. I mean, I've thought about what it would be like to be me and speak with a French accent. I'd be the most fuckable babe in L.A. But I never really wondered what it would be like to *be* French. For real. If I were French, would I still be a lawyer? Would I still be single? If I went shopping, what would I buy? How would I spend the day? And when I saw you, you seemed like a woman who had all the answers. Even if I didn't know the questions. So, on impulse I followed you and your bag."

"Here we are on your birthday and you're not drinking? That just won't do, Kia. Not if you're really trying to be French."

"Champagne it is."

Marie smiles approvingly and flags down a waiter. "*Deux champagnes, si'l vous plaît.*"

The waiter bows his head and disappears lickety-split.

"So tell me, back in America, if I had followed you today, what would I have witnessed of your life?"

"Today is what? Friday? I'd be working. It's Drew's turn to decide on lunch. Probably Indian. He loves the stuff. It being my birthday, he might spring for the Palm, an upscale restaurant a few blocks from the office. He'd order the steak; I'd get the lobster. We'd argue about who ate more of the other's meal. It's usually me, but that doesn't give him the right to call me on it."

"So, you like this Drew?"

"He's all right."

"The flicker I saw in your eye says he's a lot more than that."

I rub my eyes vigorously. "It's all this smoke. Word hasn't traveled abroad that cigarette smoking causes cancer?"

"I quit three years ago."

Everyone in France smokes. And those who don't, smoke on occasion. And those who don't admit to that—take a puff here and there. The waiter has returned with our drinks. Marie holds up her glass, urging me to do the same.

"May the flicker never fade." She clinks my glass and takes a sip.

"You don't understand. I don't like him. We work together."

"So?"

"And he's wh—" I stop myself.

I mean, I'm not a racist but if I tell this woman I don't like Drew because he's a white boy, wouldn't I sound like one? She might speak the language, but that doesn't mean she understands American social politics.

"What, Kia? He's not handsome enough for you?"

"He's cute, for a wh—"

Dang, there I go again.

"He's decent-looking enough. He's just . . . it's just . . . we work together."

That's a safe answer. A mostly truthful answer. Even if Drew were black, we share an office; it would just be too weird.

"My first husband and I were coworkers. Translators at the embassy."

Translators at the embassy. Now, that's some sexy shit. A high-profile job where no one gets hurt. I want a job like that. Heck, I want a first husband.

"Hey, I thought lovers were supposed to prevent divorces?"

"My first husband died. I don't think my lover could have prevented that."

I feel like a jackass. "Oh, I'm so sorry. Guess you were right about the Paris-foot-in-mouth thing."

"Don't be sorry. René was a wonderful man. He lived a good life. And then he decided he'd try something different."

"Is that how you view death, Marie? As just something different? Can something so encompassing really be that simplistic?"

"Kia, I don't know if there's a Heaven or Hell. I know what I believe. But I don't know anything for sure. The only thing I do know is that no matter what turns out to be the truth, death is certainly different from this. When René learned he was going to experience it a lot sooner than either of us had expected, he voted against getting ready to die and instead got ready for something different. It made it easier to bear. It still does. Just yesterday I got excited because I'd found a rare port that he liked. I actually picked up the bottle and headed to the register before I realized that he wasn't here to drink it. And before I could get sentimental and weepy, I imagined him skiing the clouds with God. And all I could do was smile."

Marie was wrong about the flicker in my eye, but I'm definitely seeing one in hers. She must've loved René an awful lot. I'm dying to hear more about the two of them, but I'm not sure where the line between curious and inappropriate meet. As if I haven't crossed it once already by following her.

"Do you still work at the embassy?"

"No, I work for my myself now. I'm a paid conversationalist. This one is going to cost you thirty euros." She holds out an empty hand to me. "And yes, I do take American Express."

She can't possibly be serious? Can she? The smirk on her face tells me she's not.

"People actually pay me to have conversations with them. CEOs trying to keep their English up to par. Actors trying to become the next American superstar. Sometimes people hire me out as an official translator. They take me on business trips, movie sets, presidential inaugurations."

I would've liked being French. Being her and being French.

She opens a small cobalt-blue case. "Cigarette?"

"Marie, I thought you quit three years ago?"

"I started back up two days later. It was a valiant effort. One that won't soon be repeated, but valiant nonetheless."

She tilts her head in order to light her cigarette, the way one might tilt their head in anticipation of being kissed. There is no doubt about it. Marie whatever her last name is was put on this earth to smoke cigarettes. The way she nestles it so gently between her index and middle finger. The way her lips pucker just so with each inhale. Smoke tumbling out her mouth like a poem on the exhale. Yep, she was born to smoke, cancer be damned.

I think back to the last time I smoked a cigarette. I wonder how Belinda is doing? Did she get another job? Did she get another man? Another knucklehead like Junior? Maybe she met a decent brother with a steady nine-to-five, the always-home-for-dinner type. Someone who doesn't just tolerate her kids but adores them. Adores her. She deserves that.

"Let me have one of those," I say, hoping they taste nothing like Belinda's Newports.

"I suppose I've kept you in suspense long enough. I'm afraid you're going to feel your adventure was somewhat in vain. I'm actually wearing what I bought."

She toys with the bag. "I make it a habit never to promise whoever I'm with that they will be my first kiss of the day or my last. But I can promise they alone will have the privilege of seeing, touching, removing whatever panties I happen to be wearing at the time. Usually I carry a spare pair in my bag, but today . . ."

She holds up a dainty little clutch. Barely enough room for her apparently bulging black book let alone a spare pair of undies.

"Today vanity overruled my pragmatic nature. I dropped by the shop to pick up a new pair before meeting my husband. We play this little game where he has to guess what color my panties are just by the feel of them. If we play it at lunch, I can guarantee he's home in time for dinner."

That's hot! I'll have to remember that little trick.

Marie looks at me pointedly. "So this bag holds the old . . ."

"Don't say it, don't say it," I beg her through my laughter.

"You, my new friend, have been chasing after a pair of dirty panties," she squeals.

"I am so pathetic. I really do need to get laid."

"What are your plans for dinner tonight?" Marie asks.

"I'm going to get all dolled up and go to Maxim's."

"Maxim's is a bust. What dolt decided to take you there?"

"No dolt. Just me. I've never gone out to dinner by myself, Marie. Breakfast and lunch, but never dinner. I thought tonight would be a perfect time to see if I could do it."

"Do you know how to use a knife and fork? Can you swallow without assistance? Of course you can do it, but women like us shouldn't have to."

"We shouldn't have to, but the fact is some of us do have to."

She reaches for her cellular. "I have the perfect dinner companion for you."

I've danced to this tune before. She's about to set me up with the only other black person she knows, probably some Congolese Muslim refugee. Never mind that we don't speak the same language or pray to the same God, we're both playing the melanin game, that should be common interest enough. The last time this happened to me I swore it was the last time it would happen to me.

"My travel agent, Barb, went through a lot of trouble to get me this reservation . . ."

"Tell her the duck was delicious," Marie says, holding up

her index finger, throwing me the apparently international *hold on* sign.

"*Bonjour, mon ami*," she says into the phone.

She proceeds to have a brief animated conversation. I make out a few of the words: *americaine, noire, belle*. While I don't object to being described as a beautiful, black American woman, I'm not feeling the idea of being set up on a blind date by a woman I barely know.

"Where are you staying?" she asks me.

"Hôtel du Louvre," I say reluctantly.

"He'll meet you in the lobby at nine."

I try to throw her an appreciative smile.

Marie covers the phone with her hand. "You don't seem too pleased."

"No, it's fine. It's just dinner, right?"

"At Alcazar, only the hottest restaurant in town. I'll have to call in a few favors to get you a reservation, but it'll be worth it. I'd love to join you two, but it's too late to get a baby-sitter."

Okay, she has a great job, a loving husband, a loving lover, and a kid? Her life certainly seems to be in order. Maybe I should give her a shot at mine?

"Marie, does he at least speak English?"

"Flawlessly. He's not quite the conversationalist that I am, but you've tripled your chances of getting laid."

"Well, then, by all means, tell him nine-thirty." I'll need the extra half-hour to get *getting-laid* ready.

She gets back on the phone and prattles on in French for another minute or two. Once that is done, I hand her one of my packages. She gleefully opens it.

"Kia, this is the pink blouse I tried on. You're giving it to me?"

"We Americans tend to play by our own rules, so I'm starting a new tradition of giving gifts on my birthday."

"I'll deny ever saying it, but I've always liked you Americans. And your traditions."

We spent the remainder of the afternoon telling tales through clouds of French cigarettes and flutes of French champagne. Needless to say, I missed my facial.

Eighteen

*The more I traveled the more I realized that fear
makes strangers of people who should be friends.*
—*Shirley MacLaine, American actress*

I CAN'T REMEMBER the last time I had a date on my birth-
day. Last year my girls and I had dinner at Table 8. The year
before that it was at Mr. Chow. And the year before that, Flash
and I were dating but I was in the middle of a tough trial, so
dinner was out. He did send a fly floral arrangement to my job,
though. Flash was always good for those grand gestures; it's just
the small ones that were out of his reach. Like remembering to
Tivo my favorite show, when he knows I'm stuck at work, in-
stead of calling me later to tell me how good it was and what a
shame it is that I missed it. The small gestures aren't as easily
remembered, but they're the ones that count. They're the ones
that keep you going until the next grand gesture comes along.

At least that's what I've decided as I'm standing in the lobby,
waiting for my date. It shouldn't be too hard for us to spot one
another, two black dots amongst an ocean of white ones.

I see a dead ringer for Ed Bradley standing by the doors,
looking around. He seems to be in reasonably good shape. A lit-
tle dated on the wardrobe, but nothing that a quick spin
through Saks couldn't handle. He catches me checking him
out. He nods and smiles warmly. I was hoping to avoid dating

the over-fifty set until I was over forty, but, hey, it's just dinner, right? I make my way over to him.

"Hi, I'm Kia," I say, extending my hand.

He seems momentarily thrown by the gesture, but quickly recovers and shakes my hand. "William."

"What a relief. You're American. I didn't need to be so nervous. At least now I know you'll get my jokes." I wait for a laugh that doesn't come. "So, um . . . I'm ready when you are."

William looks at me strangely. Just as it's beginning to dawn on me I may have the wrong guy, an attractive black woman approaches us.

"Honey, this is Kia. Kia, this is my girlfriend, Robyn," William says as his eyes dart nervously between Robyn and me.

Shaking her hand, I wonder if there is a cap on how many times you can make a fool of yourself in one day.

"It's so nice to run into another sista. We've been here for ten days and you're the first," Robyn says.

"Don't forget that group of merry widows from the cruise," William adds.

He seems relieved that Robyn is keeping her cool. Back in the States she might've acted a fool if she caught someone trying to step to her man, even mistakenly. But over here—she's just happy to see another black face. Europe will do that to you.

I'm guessing that Robyn is in her early forties. She could be me five years from now; although I'd never shop at Ann Taylor's or wear that Tiffany & Co. silver heart charm bracelet every nouveau-riche black woman feels the need to sport.

"Are you two enjoying Paris?" I ask, hoping they didn't catch me giving Robyn the once over.

"We weren't sure what to expect, considering France's take on Iraq and everything, but I can truly say this is the one time when being black has worked to our advantage," William replies.

"The other night, we actually got a better table than this white couple that arrived before us," Robyn says.

I had a similar experience while hailing a cab. Two white women, clearly American in their Wal-Mart shorts and Fantastic Sam haircuts, were in line ahead of me. The cab driver refused them and picked me up instead. The driver proceeded to deliver an anti-American tirade that I was not quite prepared for. He asked me if I voted for Bush. No. He asked me if I was for the war. No. He asked me if I was for America's pro-Israel policies. No. See, black Americans get it, he said. White Americans were confused and arrogant. I know I should have told him his attitude was grossly unfair. There were plenty of whites that felt the way I did, but it was hot and my feet hurt (Manolo Blahniks will do that to you). I was happy for the ride and my black American behind wasn't going to say anything to screw it up.

I CONTINUE MAKING small talk with Robyn and William. "You said you've been here for ten days? You must've seen an awful lot?"

"Oh yes. We've seen practically everything the city has to offer. William is a real history nut, so we get up early every morning and take some sort of tour. We've been to every museum, palace, and war memorial. Who knew a city could be so beautiful and educational? What have you and your man gotten into?"

Normally this would be an awkward moment for me, but today it's just a moment. "Oh, it's just me."

Robyn gives me a look I've seen a hundred times. The *pity you don't have a man and I do* look.

"It's okay, really. I've had the best time. Sleeping in, ordering room service. I even got a real French manicure yesterday. I've taken in the obvious sights, but mostly I've just gotten my shop on. You know how it is, girl."

She didn't have a fucking clue. It was my turn to give her a look of pity. We both know her vacation sucks compared to mine. And for the first time in a long time, me, the girl without a man, was the envy of a girl with one.

Robyn grabs a hold of William's hand. "Well, it was nice meeting you but we need to run. We don't have a reservation anywhere and I'm starving."

"I've got one at Maxim's that I'm not going to use . . ."

The look of pity is back. "I can see how dining at a place like that by yourself wouldn't be too much fun."

"I was actually looking forward to it, but my date is taking me to Alcazar instead."

"A blind date, I suppose?" William asks.

I nod and he lets out a small laugh, now understanding why I came at him the way that I did. Meanwhile, Robyn's face contorts in such a way I see that I have completely pushed her world off kilter and she is desperately trying to right it.

"How did you score reservations at two of the hottest restaurants in town on a Friday night in August?" Robyn asks.

"Who cares, if she's willing to give us one of them?" William interjects, realizing that if Robyn continues down this path I might rescind the offer I technically haven't extended yet.

Robyn is not too pleased with either of us at the moment, but a sista's need to get her grub on at a world-famous restaurant usually overrides her need to act ugly.

"The reservation is under Carson, for ten o'clock. Try the duck, I heard it's the bomb."

"This is really kind of you," William says sincerely.

"Yeah, thanks," Robyn says, not so sincerely.

As they start for the door, William turns back toward me. "You don't need to be nervous. Even if he doesn't get your jokes, he'll laugh like he does."

I smile and wave goodnight to the both of them. I check my watch. Nine-forty. Homeboy is late. Maybe he's not coming. Maybe I should've kept that Maxim's reservation. I hope I didn't get all gussied up for nothing. I'm wearing a dress I bought this afternoon: an empire waist, knee-length black chiffon dress. Very girly-girl. Very *I feel pretty. Oh, so pretty.*

I feel a tap on my shoulder. I take a deep breath and turn around.

"You must be Kia."

"Uh-huh," I say, completely dumbfounded.

I don't know why it didn't occur to me, but I can honestly say that it never crossed my mind that he would be . . . well . . . that he would be white.

He gives me a kiss, kiss, kiss. The French always feel the need to one-up everybody so I just go with it. My ringing cell interrupts the moment.

"I'm so sorry. I'll only be a minute."

He politely takes a step back, to give me the illusion of privacy. "No problem."

"Hello."

"How's my birthday girl?"

"Fine, Mom. How are you?"

"Just missing you, is all. Are you meeting any nice people?"

"As a matter fact I'm with one right now. I'm on a date."

And I'll be damned if she doesn't drop the phone.

"Mom, hello? Are you there?"

"Hi, baby!"

"Dad?"

I hear my mother saying something in the background.

"Yes, baby. Your mother wants to know his name?"

"Hold on a sec, Dad, I have to ask him."

I wish I hadn't let that one slip out, but it's too late now. I cover the phone with my hand and step toward my date.

"We've established that I'm Kia, but who exactly are you?"

"Philippe."

"His name is Philippe," I say to my dad, smiling at the sound of it.

"Philippe? What kind of name is Philippe?" my father asked.

"It's the French equivalent of Leroy, I suppose."

"Hmmm. Look at his shoes. You can tell a lot about a man by his shoes."

Philippe is wearing what I guess are tan Bruno Magli summer loafers.

"They're handsome, well-made shoes, Dad."

"He could still be frontin'. Does he have a bulge in his back pocket?"

"Um, Dad, I don't think that's where his bulge would be."

"Don't play games with me, Kia. Does it look like the boy is carrying a wallet or not?"

"Philippe, would it be terribly rude if I asked you to turn around for me?"

"Not if you're willing to do the same when asked," he replies playfully.

It takes me a moment, but sure enough I spot a slight bulge in his back pocket, and just a little bit of an ass to boot.

"That's affirmative, Dad."

"I don't know how it is that you find yourself going out with a man when you don't know his name, but go on. Just be careful. Make sure the hotel knows where he's taking you. And you call us when you get home."

"You're kidding me, right? You realize I'm celebrating my thirty-fifth birthday?"

"Until you find some other man to lay awake wondering if you got home safely, it's still my job. And I'll be happy to do it till your ninety-fifth birthday, if that's what it takes."

The best birthday gift ever.

"I love you, Daddy."

"I love you, too. And tell that boy, he's just a plane ride away from an ass whuppin' if he doesn't treat you right."

I hang up laughing, knowing that even though he hates to fly, he would jump on a plane in a heartbeat if any one harmed one of his girls. I smile at Philippe. He smiles back. He's cute for a white boy.

"*Bon anniversaire*," he says handing me a small box.

A gift-giving, cute white boy. Yippee! I open the box.

"It's beautiful."

Philippe slips a single perfect gardenia onto my wrist, tying it with a ribbon.

"A little old-fashioned, I know, but there's something about seeing a woman in a wrist corsage."

I notice his crisp white French-cuffed shirt. "I feel the same way about a man in cuff links."

"Now it's your turn."

"Excuse me?"

"It's your turn to turn around for me," he says all flirty-like.

I oblige, and after about twenty seconds I turn back around.

"I'm not finished."

I turn back around. He probably hasn't seen a bootie this big in a minute. Not too many French mommas are packing it like this.

"Okay, you can turn back around now."

"You've finished checking out my derrière?" I ask with a sexy confidence.

"No, but I don't want to miss our reservation," he says, tucking my arm into his and ushering me out the door.

WE MISSED IT. Philippe and I were so busy talking we failed to notice that the cab driver was lost. The maître d' could care less it was the driver's first day on the job or that it was my birthday. After three unsuccessful attempts to reason/cajole/bribe him, we left.

"So, what will it be? Alain Ducasse? La Coupole?"

"Is it okay if we just walk a bit and when we see something we like, we stop?"

He again wraps my arm around his. "It's more than okay."

"How do you and Marie know each other?"

"We used to work together."

"At the embassy?"

"Yes," he says flatly.

"Don't say anything to ruin the fantasy. I've decided that it's the perfect job. Nobody's life is ruined because you used the informal *you* when the formal *you* would have been more appropriate."

"It is possible to misinterpret something badly enough and start WW III."

I laugh. "That would kind of suck. But beyond that . . ."

"Beyond that, translating other people's words is mindless, dull work. It lacks creativity. Passion. Risk. Things no man should live without."

"Is there something no woman should live without?"

"A sense of herself, and a man who loves her," he replies.

I'm batting zero for two here. As we walk a bit further I suddenly spot the perfect place for us to eat.

"I know it's sacrilegious but after a week of eating French food, I can't eat another cut of veal, another order of vegetables covered in a creamy sauce, another anything with the word *fro-*

mage anywhere near it. Call me a dumb American tourist but I'm craving a Quarter Pounder."

Philippe laughs hysterically.

"As a kid, I spent plenty of birthdays here. It's sort of a Carson tradition. After shopping or a movie, there was always a birthday lunch with Mom at Mickey D's. It was the only time we ever spent just the two of us. My mother never wanted to appear like she favored my sister over me or vice versa, so it was always the three of us going here. The three of us going there. Except on our birthdays. The last time we went I was sixteen. I had just passed my driver's-license test and I was meeting Alfrazier Murray at the roller skating rink later. You couldn't tell me I wasn't the baddest thing walking."

"I take it that's a good thing?"

"It's a very good thing," I reply.

Opting for a new twist on an old tradition, we ordered burgers, fries, and champagne splits. Like I said, the French always have to one up everybody. They serve liquor at their McDonald's. Through bites of the best Quarter Pounder I've ever had, Philippe and I continued getting to know each other.

"So, what do you think of Paris?"

"What do I think of Paris or what do I think of you?"

"You have no room in your life for bullshit, have you, Kia?"

"Nope."

"That's a fine quality. Hold on to it." He smiles bashfully at me. "So, then . . . what was your first impression of me?"

I take a good long look at him and realize that he's more than cute for a white boy. He's Brad Pitt cute. George Clooney cute. White boys who transcend the cute-for-a-white-boy label.

"You remind me of a tall, perfectly chilled glass of champagne. All bubbly and golden with your blond hair and your sun-kissed skin. Very Louis Roederer—in a suit."

He seems pleased with this description. "Then that would make you Nigerian roast in a dress."

"Okay, you're an eighty-dollar bottle of champagne and I'm a ten-cent cup of coffee?"

"Coffee appeases all five senses. I dare the best champagne to do that."

I think on it for a beat. "I get the see, feel, taste, and smell. But what sound does a cup of coffee make?"

"The perfect cup will always elicit an *ahh*." He closes his eyes on the *ahh* . . .

I like being described as an *ahh*! Philippe feeds me one of his French fries. I've long since polished off mine. I catch a glimpse of his cuff link. Multicolored mosaic tile squares. With what little I know of him I'd say they suit him perfectly: bold and whimsical.

Philippe catches me staring. "A gift from an old flame."

"She has good taste."

"She's a nut. A kleptomaniac to be exact. I seem to have a weakness for women who are destined to end up in jail."

"Guess we're destined to be just friends then."

"Don't count me out as a lover just yet. I said it was a weakness, not an obsession." He feeds me another fry. "You mentioned earlier that you have a thing for cuff links. What's the attraction?"

"Men who wear them tend to think outside of the box. They're daring. They may not be leaders, but they're comfortable forging their own path and having no one follow."

"I assume your father is a cuff-link man?"

"My mother would always put them on for him. They'd stand close enough so he could smell her hair. She'd fasten his cuffs, then straighten his tie. Then she'd say, 'You're looking mighty fine there, Mr. Carson.' He'd reply, 'You, too, Mrs. Carson.' And then they'd kiss. My mom would always pull away first, afraid she would *rile* dad up before work. Can't have that. He'd tap her on the backside and she'd scurry off all girly and giggly. I must've watched that scene play out a hundred times while growing up. Each time marveling at the romance of it all."

"So, you've been waiting your whole life for a man to ask you to cuff him?"

I toss out a wink. "I've cuffed many a man before. Just not to his shirt."

"I read somewhere that the heart beats strongest at the wrist. Maybe that's the attraction for the both of us."

"Maybe . . ." I say, giving the sentiment serious consideration.

"I see now that you have the face of a muse, the heart of a romantic, hiding in the body of a realist. Not too many men are up for such a challenge."

"Please, Philippe, I'm hardly all of that."

"You want a man who pays the bills while wearing a smoking jacket."

"Don't be ridiculous."

"Is that an American version of a denial?"

"Fine. I'm still single because I'm looking for something that doesn't exist."

"I never said he didn't exist, Kia. Just that he would be hard to find. You may have to search the world over for a guy like that."

"Luckily, I'm not afraid to fly."

"Tell me something you *are* afraid of."

"A few days ago, Philippe, I could've given you a laundry list. But I'm trying really hard right now not to be afraid of anything."

"Fearless and sexy. An unbeatable combination, for sure."

I smile bashfully. I'll take being called sexy over pretty any day of the week. Pretty comes with the genes. Sexy is something a woman acquires all on her own.

"And what about you? Have you found *her* yet, Philippe?"

"I've been in love quite a few times. Engaged once."

"What happened?"

"She was a very passionate girl. A pyromaniac to be exact. She torched my car. The flames from that ignited another car. She's in prison now."

"Most of the world's greatest visionaries spent time in jail. Socrates, Gandhi, King, Mandela. Your girl could get out and become the next president of France," I say.

"Then I'm glad she's out of my life. The only thing worse than a convict is a politician."

People usually say lawyer, so he gets no argument from me.

"How do you feel about jazz, Kia?"

"I'm generally in favor of it."

"I feel the very same about you."

"That's not exactly a ringing endorsement, Philippe."

"The night's still young," he says, feeding me his last fry.

Nineteen

To awaken quite alone in a strange town is one of
the pleasantest sensations in the world.
    —*Freya Stark, English adventurer and author*

OH, MY HEAD HURTS. Oh, my down there hurts.

Why would my down there hurt? Don't tell me I finally had
sex and I don't even remember it. That's what I get for drink-
ing all that champagne. Oh, and scotch. After midnight I
started drinking scotch.

What is that awful smell? I struggle to take in air. Tabasco?
I pry my eyes open and find a glass of red liquid sitting on the
nightstand of my hotel room. It's not only the smell but also the
sight of it that is making me sick. I glance at the clock. It's one-
thirty in the afternoon.

I turn away from the drink and close my eyes. Wait, maybe
my cooch doesn't hurt? Maybe . . . yeah, it's just my thong
crammed up into places no thong should go. I adjust the of-
fending article and . . . *voilà*! It's now just a dull headache that
is keeping me from feeling human again.

My eyes pop back open. Hey, does that mean I didn't
have sex?

I glance at the empty space next to me. It's clear nobody but
me has slept in this bed. I notice my dress from last night is
slung neatly over a chair in the corner, but I don't remember

taking it off. I see that I've slept in my robe, which I don't remember putting on.

Hmmm. Philippe must've brought me back here, undressed me, and put me to bed. But he didn't sleep with me? What's up with that? There was definitely some chemistry between us. There should've been sex. Birthday plus fine man plus alcohol equals sex. Everybody knows that.

Come on, Kia. Think. I remember meeting up with three of Philippe's friends at a jazz club. Le Petit something or other. A cool spot where they played real jazz, not that 94.7 The Wave Kenny G crap, but the stuff Charlie Parker and company would have been proud to listen to.

And there was weed. Good weed. Good make-you-forget-everything-you-ever-knew weed. I remember sitting in the club, Philippe holding my left hand and a big fatty planted firmly in my right. Oh, how I miss getting high.

I haven't smoked in years. Random drug testing at work always had me too scared to hit it the few times it's been offered to me since graduating law school. That should be reason enough for me to tell Holden to go screw himself. *No drug testing in private practice . . .*

There was laughing. I remember lots of laughing. Laughing till I damn near peed on myself. Maybe that's why we didn't have sex? No, no, I definitely would remember if I'd peed on myself. But what was so funny? What am I talking about? We were all high. Nothing could have been funny and we would've thought it was funny. It was just that kind of night. Me, Philippe, and his friends, drinking, smoking, talking, laughing like we had known each other for ages. Ooh, and I remember us *arguing* like we'd known each other for ages, too. Something about the war. It's always about the war over here. I think Philippe said, "Americans are imperialistic bullies." I reminded him, "The French invented the word. Napoleon, anyone?"

Instead of being offended, he actually complimented me, saying "How rare it is to find an American who understands that the world was larger than fifty states." I had to agree with him there. Only sixteen percent of Americans own a passport. It seems we have a strong desire to rule the world; we just don't want to travel it.

That's when I began dissing America. Something about the racism, the bureaucracy, Big Brother constantly looking over your shoulder. Then Philippe started dissing France. Something about the racism, the bureaucracy, Big Brother constantly looking over your shoulder. That led us right back to the war. The French don't want to fight in it, but they can't stop talking about it. I think it was his friend Gerrard. No, no it was the pudgy one. Uh, uh . . . Jean-Paul. Jean-Paul said, "America is a country full of nothing but war-mongering, bad-filmmaking barbarians."

I pointed out something to the effect that "Yes, Hollywood has been in a slump, but at least we're making bad *happy* films. I find great comfort in escaping into a world where the good guy always wins, the bad guy always ends up in jail, and the girl always gets her man. Sure, it's bullshit, but so what? Only the French would go to a movie looking for the meaning of life. The rest of us are just there for the buttered popcorn and the Red Vines. As for our war mongering, yeah, we're wrong for being in Iraq, but France is wrong for not being there. If they are so morally opposed to what we're doing, they should be fighting side by side with the Iraqis. Opposing the war, but not doing anything about it . . . it's like being the one guy in the frat house who knows better so he doesn't participate in the gang rape of a sorority girl, but refuses to come to her aid. In France, such cowardice may warrant a Nobel Peace Prize, but in America it can land you two years in jail."

Ouch! That wasn't very nice. A sober me would've never said anything like that, especially without having any of my crew there to me back up. *Dumb, Kia. Very dumb*. I can see why I didn't get any. He probably brought my dumb ass back to the hotel right after that. Game over. Thanks for playing.

Only . . . after that I remember reggae. At least I think there was reggae. Yes, there was definitely reggae, and more weed. Weed is probably the reason I didn't get a proper beat down for speaking badly about the French on their turf. Philippe and his friends were either too high to understand what I said or too high to care.

At the reggae spot there was more laughing, more drinking, Red Stripes, and awkward attempts to speak with a Jamaican accent. Nothing is funnier than a drunk, stoned, white Frenchman trying to talk like a black Rastafarian. *That* I definitely remember.

Yes, it's all coming back to me now. Around sunup we'd had enough. Philippe's friends jumped into one cab, we jumped into another. I remember rolling the window down and a gentle Parisian breeze caressing my face. It felt like a kiss from Heaven. Oh. My. God! There was kissing. Not on the lips. On the inside of my wrist. Oh, and it made me wetter than April. I don't think I'll ever be able to put perfume on my wrist again without thinking about that kiss. Philippe kissed my wrist and right when things started to heat up, the cab had to pull over because I had to . . . throw up.

A universal, unequivocal sex buster.

I close my eyes but my headache has worsened. Maybe that's what the Tabasco drink is for? To cure my hangover? Reaching for the glass, I see that an envelope with my name on it sits underneath.

I stare at the envelope. I want to burn it as much as I want to read it. What does one say in a letter to a person they have known for only a few hours? A loudmouth, sloppy-drunk kind of person. Burn it. I should definitely burn it.

I take a sip of the red concoction. The horrible smell is almost strong enough to overpower the disgusting taste. It was sweet of Philippe to go to so much trouble to order this from room service, though. I guess the least I could do is hear him out. What the hay? I've gone up against murderers and rapists, I can handle a bad review. I rip the envelope open.

Dearest Kia,

I trust this letter finds you well enough to recall the merriment of last night. If not, I assure you that you were a complete delight and held on to your dignity till the very end. I was particularly impressed with the way you managed to purge without getting anything on your dress or shoes. A sign of a true lady.

It is with a sad heart that I leave you sleeping soundly and alone. It is probably for the best, though, as I am scheduled to leave for Dubai today on my August holiday. Any more time spent with you might have found me postponing a trip I have spent a year planning. As they say in the movies, though, We'll always have Paris.

I take with me vivid memories of a passionate, intelligent, lovely woman who holds the world in her hand, and I hope a bit of France in her heart.

So, while lovers we have yet to be (I remain eternally optimistic), friends I hope we always are. The world is a far less daunting place when beautiful friends are scattered throughout it.

Philippe

Only one thought races through my mind: Where the hell is Dubai, and how long will it take me to get there? Naw, I'm not that hard up for sex. Close, though.

I grab my journal and return to bed. Looking back on the

crazy events of last night, I am struck by the randomness of it all. A black girl from Ladera hanging out with three white boys from Paris as though it was the most natural thing in the world. The things we had in common—our need to love and be loved, our need to be understood, or at the very least accepted—far outnumbered the things we didn't share. In America, I'm constantly aware of the black and white of things, be it people or the law. But last night I was able to transcend some of that, and today somehow I feel lighter for it.

My head feeling slightly better, I order a croissant and coffee and decide to spend the rest of the day lying in bed, doing absolutely nothing at all.

Twenty

✈

Every exit is an entry somewhere else.
—*Tom Stoppard, English playwright*

"MADEMOISELLE, you have a visitor waiting for you in the lobby," the front desk clerk has just rung my room to say.

My heart quickens a bit. Maybe Philippe missed his flight? No, he probably just sent Jean-Paul over to check on me.

"Is he a tall cutie or more the potbellied variety?"

"He's definitely a tall cutie," she replies, a bit too lustfully.

"I'll be down in a minute."

I hang up and race into the bathroom to brush my teeth and wash my face. Before running out of the door, I throw on a hand-beaded by Lotte camisole and a pair of jeans. It's important to be quick, but more so to be cute.

What if Philippe didn't miss his flight at all but actually rearranged his trip? Who knew I had pull like that? Up till now, I couldn't get a man to rearrange his tee-off time, let alone his entire vacation. I must remember to write down everything I said or did since the moment we met.

Luckily the elevator ride down to the lobby is an express trip. I flit back and forth in the busy lobby, searching for Philippe. Not finding him anywhere, I head for the front desk.

"Excuse me, I just got a call saying I had a visitor waiting for me?"

"Yes, mademoiselle."

"I've looked all over the lobby . . ."

"Not all over," I hear a sexy mothafucka say.

I turn to see Mr. Grand Gesture himself, standing there with a Cheshire grin on his face.

"Happy Birthday!" Flash says.

"My birthday was yesterday."

He produces a sweet bouquet of country flowers from behind his back. "Better late than not at all."

Ohh, he makes me so mad. There was a time when I would've killed to have this moment, and now that I could give a hoot, here he is.

"Let me get this straight. I ask you to come to Paris with me and you say no. You ask to come to Paris with me and I say no. And what happens? You fucking come to Paris?"

"I hate it when people tell me no."

"Yeah, Flash, well so do I."

"You want my arm to fall off or what?"

Flash is quoting Billie Dee's classic line from *Lady Sings the Blues*. One of my favorite movies of all time. I take the dang flowers and smile. How could I not? I can't remember the last time I received flowers from a man, and now all of a sudden I've got them coming out of my ass.

"How did you find me?"

"I called Diane at her office, told her I wanted to wish you a happy birthday."

"Calling would've been cheaper."

"Yes, but then I wouldn't be able to do this . . ."

Flash plants an old-fashioned Hollywood-style kiss on me. With a dip and everything. Diane was right. It was just my ego talking when I said I no longer had feelings for Flash. I can't lay claim to what exactly my feelings are, but that kiss definitely has me feeling something. I begin walking toward the elevator.

"Well, come along, then," I say, trying to sound unaffected.

"I don't know why you're acting like you're not happy to see me."

Therein lies the irony of the moment. I was happy to see him. And it pissed me off.

Twenty-one

Sometimes the road less traveled is less traveled for a reason.
—*Jerry Seinfeld, American comedian*

"KIA, look at the composition of this piece. It's amazing how the artist is able to draw the eye to both the foreground and the background."

"Mm-hmm," I say.

I'm bored out of my skull. I'm reminded of my encounter with Robyn and William and tales of their dull orchestrated vacation. I'm feeling her pain now.

Surprise, surprise. Flash and I have spent the day at not just one museum, mind you, but three of them. The first one I actually enjoyed: a photo exhibit featuring five amateur photographers armed only with digital cameras who spent twenty-fours hours capturing a-day-in-the-life photos. Big mistake on my part. Flash has fallen under the illusion that I was now an art aficionado and would enjoy spending the entire afternoon inside cold air-conditioned rooms looking at artworks I can't afford and wouldn't buy even with someone else's money. It might not have been so bad if he could've just chilled out and let me view the installations at my own pace, lost in my own thoughts. But no, he wanted to discuss (it's a one-sided discussion, since he's doing all the talking), interpret, and analyze every photo, painting, and sculpture we come across. And we've come across many. We're currently viewing a nature retrospective. Snoresville.

Flash points to a photograph. "Oh, check this one out. See how the use of light gives this piece texture?"

"Very Ansel Adams," I say.

I regret the words the second they tumble out.

"Are we even looking at the same picture, Kia?"

"Yes, Flash. It's a black-and-white photo of a tree."

"It's nothing like Ansel Adams' work."

"You're right. Can we go now? In case you didn't notice, I stopped having fun like four hours ago." I've just reached my breaking point.

"I noticed. I just thought you'd get past it. Excuse me for trying to share my passion with you." Flash has clearly just reached his.

"Somehow it never feels like sharing. It feels like a lecture. As your girlfriend I put up with it because I thought that's what girlfriends are supposed to do. But bootie-call credo number nine clearly frees me from those sorts of girlfriend obligations."

"I was just trying to help you become a more well-rounded person."

"If you want to tell me a story about an artist who rushed to finish his painting before his bout with Parkinson's disease made it impossible for him to hold a steady brush—do it because you think it's a story I might enjoy hearing, not because you're trying to turn me into your idea of a well-rounded person. I admit I could use some help in that area, but I'd like it to come from someone who actually embodies the quality."

"What are you trying to say, Kia?"

"No offense, but you're about as well-rounded as a fork. You know a lot about art, I'll give you that. But tell me, how many nations are there in the European Union? How about something a little closer to home? Can you even name the two senators from California? Did you even bother to study the issues and vote in the last election?"

I know the answer is no. Flash doesn't believe in the political process. And that always bothered me about him. I guess one can argue that Martin, Malcolm, Medgar, and the rest of them battled the devil for the right to vote, not the obligation. But personally, I find that to be a cop-out. Not voting is a sign of disrespect for all that our civil rights warriors fought and died for. If the white man knew what voting slackers blacks folks would become, they would've granted us the privilege from the start, and then Martin, Malcolm, and Medgar would still be alive today.

"So instead of dealing with the real issue here, Kia, you're just going to kick mud on my new white sneaks."

"I'm just trying to make a point, Flash. Well-rounded means multifaceted. Not just being well versed in the shit *you* happen to be interested in."

I must've made a direct hit with that one, because for the first time all day homeboy is speechless. God bless the silence. Flash studies his museum pamphlet.

"There is just one more wing I'd like to see. Can we check it out and then we can go to Chanel or Gucci or wherever it is you'd like to go?"

"I don't want to shop. I want to chill out. Have a glass of wine. Maybe catch the sunset. Do your thing here and when you're finished, meet me at Les Deux Magots. I read somewhere that Ernest Hemingway used to hang out there."

"You're going to leave me here and go to some restaurant to chill?"

"Yep."

Flash is speechless once again. I put on my Chanel *I can ignore you because I can't really see you* sunglasses and sashay away. I don't have to look back to know that Flash is watching every step I make toward the door.

I'M POLISHING off my second glass of merlot and my first cigarette when Flash strolls into the restaurant. I can't help but laugh as I look at my watch. It's been all of thirty minutes. If I had agreed to stay at the museum, we'd have been there till closing time. But since I bailed and told him to take his time, here he is. Typical.

"When did you take up smoking?" he asks.

"Yesterday."

"It's a disgusting habit."

"Relax, Flash, it's not a habit. It's just what Europeans do. I figured if you can't beat 'em . . ."

"Join them in getting lung cancer?"

"I shared my bottle of wine with this cute little old couple in town from Provençe, and they offered me a cigarette. How could I say no?"

The couple was adorable. I had never bought into the concept that two become one when they jointly say the words *I do*, but these two moved in such tandem with one another, it made me wish that I did.

"Kia, you don't have a problem telling me no when you don't want to do something."

"Look, I'm sorry I blew up at you. But for two weeks now, it's been Kia's world. I've done exactly what I wanted to do on my vacation. You're here for all of five minutes and before I know it—my vacation has turned into your vacation. And it's not even entirely your fault. It's just what happens when we get together."

Flash lets out a surprising laugh. "Yeah, that is kind of fucked up. I should've asked you what you wanted to do today. I'm sorry. I was just so excited to show you what I love most about Paris."

"It's all good. I got to catch the sunset, and I really did enjoy the first exhibit."

Flash laughs again.

"Let me guess, that was your least favorite?"

"Kia, we always were yin and yang."

I laugh. "More like Ali and Frazier."

"But Ali and Frazier never made up. We make up very well."

Flash grabs my glass of wine from out of my hand and takes a sweet sip.

I sigh softly. "Yeah, I suppose we do."

"You going to tell me about him?"

"Who?"

"The guy you were looking for in the lobby, Kia?"

"What guy?"

"Not that game again?"

"What game?"

"The avoid-answering-the-question-by-asking-more-questions game."

"What are you talking about, Flash?"

"See what I'm saying?"

"No," I say, knowing all too well what he's saying.

"I know you weren't expecting to see me, but you almost seemed disappointed."

"I wasn't disappointed per se."

"Oh no, you didn't bring out the *per se*," he teases.

"His name is Philippe."

"Philippe? They've got brothas out here named Philippe?"

"He's not a brotha."

"What? All that mess you and your girls talk about black men dating white girls and you're out here trippin' the white fantastic?"

"Maybe if *you all* weren't so busy making a career of it, I wouldn't have been tempted . . ."

"Don't put that on me. I don't do pink toes."

"You mean to tell me, Flash, you've never slept with a white girl?"

"As a rule, I don't do pink toes. There are always exceptions."

"Well, Philippe was almost my exception," I counter.

"Is he the one that sent you the flowers?"

"The gardenia?"

"No, Kia. The overdone bouquet."

"Stop hating. The lilies were perfect. And they're from Drew."

"What's that all about? A guy doesn't send something like that unless he's campaigning."

"Don't be stupid. The boy sent me flowers for my birthday and because . . . well . . . I got suspended."

"No shit?"

"No shit."

"You got any 'fuck you' money saved up?"

"I'm kind of blowing it all on this vacation, Flash."

"You should quit anyway."

"Yeah, I was just telling someone that in my dream life I'm the black Kate Spade."

"The purse lady?" Flash asks.

"Yep. I'm actually a decent seamstress. At least I used to be. I don't know if I ever told you this, but I made most of my own clothes in high school. Even started a little business, making backpacks out of old blue jeans. Made enough money to buy my first car. A used white hard-top Mustang 5.0."

"Hey, I could shoot your catalogues for you."

"Excuse me?"

"If you quit working at the DA's office and decide to design purses, I could shoot your catalogues."

It's not enough that he's horned in on my vacation, now he has to be a part of my dream life as well?

"Think about it. The world has way too many lawyers and not enough artists."

"You sure didn't feel that way when you got pulled over by the police last year. And my useless law degree stopped them from hauling your black ass to jail."

"You've got a point there," he says with a slight chuckle.

"I thought I might," I chuckle back.

"Contrary to what you might think, Kia, I just want you to be happy. It's all I ever wanted."

It's moments like this that remind me why he's still in my life. Flash fights back a smile.

"What's so funny?" I ask.

"Earlier, you said *almost*."

"What?"

"You said Philippe was *almost the exception*. You must be jonesing right now. Being in Paris and not getting any?"

I cross my legs afraid my cooch might talk and give me away. "Naw, I'm cool."

"How long has it been, Kia?"

"It's been a minute."

I'm too embarrassed to admit that he was in fact my last. Two and a half months ago.

"It'd be a shame for you to have spent all this time in the city of love, surrounded by lovers, and not getting the chance to be one of them," he says.

"As we've just discussed, I've got bigger problems than that . . ."

"Are the answers to your other problems staring you right in the face?"

He shoots me a sexy smile. I fend mine off. I'm not ready to give in to his charms just yet.

"I didn't come all this way to fight with you. Especially when you're looking so good. Those braids are really working for you."

He puts his hand on the back of my head, grabbing a few of them. "Just think, you won't have to worry about sweating your hair out."

Flash knows all too well, horny or not, on the days when I get my hair done and maybe a day or two after, I am not sweating my hair out for anybody.

"Flying across the Atlantic is a lot of effort and expense to go through, just for some ass . . ." I point out.

"Never underestimate the power of really good ass. They put a polite spin on it, but I guarantee you it wasn't Helen of Troy's face that launched those thousand ships."

He's speaking the truth there.

"Seriously, though. Flash, why did you come here?"

"To get away. To check out the Paris art scene. To see you."

"That's sweet, but what does it mean?"

"Kia, I know we're not always good together. But we do have our moments. Maybe this is one of them. Who knows? Maybe this moment stretches into a lifetime of moments. Maybe not. Maybe it's just an isolated chunk of time that two people who care about each other spend together in a romantic city doing romantic things, mostly in bed. Either way, it was worth the time, effort, and expense."

He tugs a little harder on my hair, biting his lip, like he does just before he cums. Damn him! Flash could talk the panties off a nun. Forty minutes later mine were on the floor.

The foreplay was adequate. Not quite the showstopper it's

been in the past, but there was no need to panic. There was still the finale to look forward to. I tried to keep focused on the task at hand but somehow my thoughts kept drifting to everything but. What's wrong with me? Didn't I ask for this? To get laid, that is. Why am I not into it? Why am I thinking about what I wrote in my journal earlier today?

Since it's all everyone keeps saying they want for me, I've been thinking quite a bit about what it would take to make me happy. I've narrowed it down to three things:

1. A job where I can give back to the community.

I know how fortunate I am to have been brought up in a loving, two-parent home where I never wanted for anything. I've never been homeless. I've never been hungry. I've never ever really been scared. Scared that I might be shot in my sleep by a random bullet meant for someone else. Scared that my whole life was going to boil down to attending second-rate schools, wearing secondhand clothes, receiving Third World medical care, in a country that prides itself on being first. That's what life is for many black Americans. As one of the lucky ones, I owe them a shot at something better.

Maya is committed to making films that show positive black images. That's her way of giving back. Diane believes a smile is the most powerful possession a person has. She takes patients who have no insurance, sometimes letting them barter for her services. Her gardener and housekeeper are working off a root canal and upper bridgework at this very moment. That's her way of giving back.

I want to change the world one case at a time. Oh, and I want to look good while doing it. Chic altruism is the only life for me.

2. Travel the world.

I want to keep exposing myself to new people, new ideas, and new ways of thinking. It's easy for me to lose perspective in

L.A. Everyone I know there thinks and lives the way I do. It's comforting, but rarely challenging.

And I realize I don't want to just get laid . . .

3. I want to fall in love.

I want to fall in love with a man who has passion for life and for me. A God-fearing man who can keep me on my path when I lose my way. A man who can make me laugh. A man who can help me grow in ways I'd never imagined. A man who makes me feel beautiful from the inside out. And a man who can kiss. It's all about the kiss. Slow, lingering, make-you-think-about-changing-your-last-name kisses.

Flash's kisses used to do it for me. But now . . . now nothing. I'm beginning to see that God wasn't keeping Flash in my life for any particular reason. I was. I kept him around, not because I thought he was The One, but because he was Someone at a time when I was afraid there might be No One. But Someone just isn't good enough anymore. Especially now that I know that being with no one can be cool, too.

As if he can hear my thoughts, Flash suddenly rolls off of me.

He smiles sheepishly. "I'm sorry, Kia, I must be jet-lagged."

I look down to see his soft penis swimming in a now too-large condom.

"That's not it and you know it."

"Hey, you're the one who just celebrated a birthday, not me."

"It's not an age thing, either."

"All right, so what is it, then?" He sounds far more frustrated than curious.

"I've said this to you before, but this time I really mean it. We've outgrown the bootie-call thing. We've outgrown each other."

Flash hops up to flush the condom down the toilet. "Come on, Kia, this sort of thing happens all the time with all couples."

"But we're not a couple. We're fuck buddies."

"Why are you being so dramatic about this? I just need a nap."

He climbs back into bed and has the nerve to act like the conversation is over.

"Flash, you're not hearing me. Someone recently told me that I hold the world in my hand. Do you know what that means? That means everything I want is within my grasp. So why am I settling for an occasional gallon of skim milk when I can have the whole damn cow?"

"Maybe having the whole cow is greedy."

"Maybe settling for less is just needy," I counter.

I watch Flash contemplate his next move. No matter how you slice it, relationships are an emotional chess match.

"Kia, you are one of the least needy women I know. I'm sorry if I come off like I'm always trying to teach you something. I'm really just searching for something I can offer you. Something more meaningful than a good fuck. You deserve all the world has to offer. I'm just sorry you think I'm not the right man to give it to you."

He went for a bold yet vulnerable move. And he'll always have a special place in my heart because of it. I lay my head on his chest, knowing it could well be for the last time. I'm surprised by the lack of sadness I feel. I guess when you know, you know.

"I leave in the morning for Mykonos . . ."

My words hang in the air like a pair of abandoned tennis shoes dangling from a telephone wire.

Flash begins to tenderly stroke my head. "Can't wait to hear all about it. Over lunch."

"I've never been to Greece . . ."

With nothing left to say to each other, we fall fast asleep.

Mykonos

Twenty-two

> . . . A foreign country is not designed to make you comfortable. It is designed to make its own people comfortable.
>
> —*Clifton Fadiman, critic and American radio host*

SOMEBODY SHOULD have warned me.

They should have warned me that catching a cab in Mykonos is harder than catching a man. There are only fifty-eight of them serving the entire island. That may be overkill in the dead of winter when nobody is here, but it's merely an ant on an elephant's rump at the height of the tourist season.

They should've warned me that once I caught a cab I'd have to share it with three total strangers, one of whom hasn't showered in, say . . . ever, making it the single most expensive and unpleasant bus ride I've ever had.

They should have warned me that my luggage, my extremely expensive but worth every penny Tumi luggage, packed with all my European treasures would be strapped to the roof of said cab with twine used in the Peloponnesian War. And while said twine did keep my luggage from falling off, it didn't prevent birds from crapping all over it.

They should have warned me that once I arrived at my destination, I would be dropped off like a hitchhiker on the side of the road and would have to carry my bags, all three of them, down a very steep hill.

They should have warned me that my five-star hotel didn't

have bellboys or doormen or any-fucking-body who could help me carry my heavy, crapped-on bags to my room.

They should have warned me that my English–Greek dictionary would be as useful as a philosophy degree. While I could *bonjour* and *merci* my way through most situations in Paris, nothing doing here. The only Greek I can pronounce is *Alpha Phi Alpha* (I dated one in college) and *Opa!* (from *My Big Fat Greek Wedding*). I don't know what the word means, but it's supposed to be used during happy occasions, which, quite frankly, I have yet to experience since my arrival.

They should have warned me that the Greeks stare. And stare. And stare. Maybe they stare because they've never seen a black person up close. But they've got MTV over here, so they know we exist. Hell, Homer's *Odyssey*, written circa 850 B.C., has a character named Eurybates who was dark-skinned and wooly-haired, so it's not as if the concept of black folks is new to them. And yet, they stare.

They should've warned me that the streets in Mykonos don't intersect; they converge. They don't run in the standard north/south meets east/west fashion, they sort of meet up in a bizarre bureaucratic game of Twister. The streets were designed to run in a mazelike fashion to disconcert and disorient marauders. First Mediterranean pirates, later the Nazis, and later still, tourists like me. What was a ten-minute walk from my hotel into town became an hour-and-a-half walk back as I got lost over and over and over again.

They should have warned me that I'm not allowed to throw toilet paper into the toilet. It's supposed to go into the trash. The plumbing system here is extremely antiquated and just can't handle it. Just so we're clear, it doesn't matter if you wipe your nose, your cooch, or your ass, it goes in the trash. Where it sits all day until the cleaning lady comes to remove it. Talk about a society resting on its laurels. So friggin' what that the Greeks built the Acropolis, a crowning achievement of architectural vision and mastery. That was twenty-five hundred years ago, people; what have you done for me lately? Try building a toilet that flushes TOILET PAPER!

They should have warned me that all of the cute guys here are gay. And not just gay, but openly, madly in love, everywhere you look there's two of them hugged-up gay. I've got nothing against it, but I'm getting tired of being odd man out everywhere I go.

Somebody should have warned me that Greece sucks.

Twenty-three

> I might be going to hell in a bucket, but at least I'm enjoying the ride.
> —*Bob Weir, American songwriter*

MY OPTIONS WERE as follows: I could either ride a crowded bus with hundreds of eyes staring at me for the twenty-minute ride to the beach, or I could rent a moped. I foolishly opted to rent a moped.

It turns out that people, cars, mopeds, and donkeys (yes, donkeys) all travel on the same streets. There are no stoplights, no road markings, no sidewalks, no cops, nothing that would help to keep some semblance of order on these narrow, winding, ill-paved roads. I'm cautiously motoring my way to the beach, getting honked and cursed at by all those passing me by. An eighty-some-year-old man blows past me on his bicycle and I still feel as though I'm caught up in a NASCAR event. I tried to rent a helmet but the saleslady just laughed at me. I thought maybe she misunderstood, so I reached for my still completely useless Greek translation guide, and that only made her laugh harder. She explained that her English was fine, but that nobody in Greece wears helmets. It cuts down on the fun. I countered that so did being in a coma, but she didn't get the joke.

I'm trying to decide if it's safer to ride in the middle of the street or close to the edge. It boils down to: Is it better to get run over by a speeding car or be driven off a cliff by one? Either way, the extra travel insurance I bought should cover the expense of flying my dead body home.

A man in a Citroën yells expletives at me as he speeds past with his toddler son plopped in his lap. The Greeks don't believe in car seats or seatbelts, either.

Everything in me wants to turn around and go back to my hotel. The Semeli has a small, sexy pool where I can catch some sun, do some reading, and live to see another day. But I'm not a quitter and I refuse to go out like a punk. It may be sundown when I get there, but I'm going to get there. Keeping my eyes wide open, I ask God to cover me as I putt-putt all the way to Super Paradise Beach.

THE PLACE IS aptly named.

The entire beach is wired with a bumping sound system playing nothing but the hottest house, hip-hop, and R&B mixes. No need to struggle with headphones or worry about fading batteries—the DJ is handling it like I programmed the selections myself.

Alcohol is permitted on the beach. In what clearly must be a European thing, you have to get up and get the drink yourself from the bar instead of waiters bringing them to you. But at least you don't have to camouflage the alcohol by pouring it into a Coke can like we do in L.A.

And best of all . . . big booties rule the roost. Skinny girls need not apply. At first I thought I'd spotted two sistas getting into the water. All I could see was dark skin and big butts. But when they got out, their hooknoses and bone-straight roots said they weren't of the sista hood but rather the *gineka* hood, and every eye in the joint was on them. And it's not because they were butt-naked, either. Everyone here is pretty much going au naturel. That is, everyone but me. I'm sunning in my tangerine bikini, matching sarong, Kangol hat, and Jackie O. glasses. I'm looking fabulous, albeit thoroughly overdressed.

First of all, there is the staring issue to contend with. If they stare with my clothes on, I can only imagine what will happen when I'm naked. I can see it now; the tide will cease to flow, the music will come to a screeching halt, a hush will fall over the place, and what up to now has just been stares will turn into pointing and gawking. If I were twenty I might be able to handle it, my stomach was flat and my tits stood at attention. And while I'm not ashamed of my body—I'm still holding it down for an old broad—my once perky B's are starting to look like B-minuses.

My mother warned me to stay out of the sun, said it causes cancer and wrinkles, hence the hat and glasses. She pestered me to floss, said it prevents gum disease. But she never said word one that letting the *girls* hang loose and free in skimpy halter tops would someday cause my nipples to play patty-cake with my belly button. She mentioned it was tacky and not very lady-like, to which I promptly replied, "So," under my breath, of course. But she never said jack about gravity. In my cute string-bikini top, they're sitting up pretty nice, but if I take my top off and lie down, forget about it.

Greek women, however, seem to be completely comfortable with their bodies. Their hefty, potbellied, dimpled-behind, saggy-breasted bodies. I've only seen one woman with fake tits, and I'm pretty sure she was Italian.

Why is it that Europeans are comfortable with nudity and Americans are so freaked out about it? We'd rather watch someone get their head bashed in than see a bare breast on TV. And when we do choose to see a breast, it's the fake kind, sitting on top of a concave stomach and a prepubescent, waxed pussy. Real women don't look like that. Real women have stretch marks. They have soft bellies and hair (only, not under the arms or on the legs, that's just nasty). Real women don't pay thousands of dollars, risking death, to have some crackpot suck fat out of their thighs. Real women eat real food and have the curves to prove it. Real women live in Greece.

Screw it. So what if they stare? Reminiscent of my first public shower in seventh-grade PE, I take my top off quickly and roll over onto my stomach. Total breast exposure time: 0.4 seconds.

Why am I being such a chicken about this? Because Lorna warned me that such behavior will lead to unwanted attention from boys. Girls who run around topless get raped. But the truth is, grandmas get raped. Librarians get raped. Good girls get raped. While it's probably not wise for a black woman to run around topless at a Klan rally, it should be okay to do it on a nude beach.

I take a deep breath and roll over, listening for any sudden whispering. None. No laughs or giggles either. The sun feels amazing on my skin, like I've just taken a cool shower and now I'm wrapped in a towel right out of the dryer. I lie like that for an hour. Not a care in the world. This is what it means to be on vacation. No schedule to follow. No cell phone to answer. Nothing but the sun, the sand, and the sea.

I decide to go for a swim. I must be feeling myself because I can't really swim. I'm sort of a wade-in-the-water type. I used to love to take baths when I was kid. I could play in there for hours. Hiding in the bubbles, splish-splashing around. I never take baths anymore. Who has the time? Who wants to scour the bathtub beforehand and then clean it again afterwards? But that's what the Aegean Sea reminds me of—a giant warm and calming bathtub. No sharks, no seaweed, no rocks, no murk. Just a thousand bathtime buddies to keep you company.

Every woman should have this experience. To swim topless in the Aegean. I've never felt more feminine. More empowered. I've decided to forgive Greece. She was just playing hard to get. If I were her, that's how I'd play it, too. Really, what other choice does she have? If she opens her arms willingly to everyone, then before you know it, they'll turn this place into a water park. An H$_2$EuroDisneyO. There'll be a Starbucks on every corner (okay, one Coffee Bean wouldn't be so bad).

As I stroll back to my beach chair, my margarita, and my French *Vogue*, I realize that I've spent the entire day by myself, alone but not lonely. And I couldn't be happier about it. *On doit profiter*, indeed.

✈

Twenty-four

The real voyage of discovery consists not in seeing
new landscapes, but in having new eyes.
—*Marcel Proust, French author*

"OH, this is so much better than a picture."

I'm being awakened from the most delightful nap by an
eerily familiar voice. Only that's impossible because I don't
know anyone here. I lift my hat off my eyes.

"Awww!!!" I scream, like Freddie Kruger's chasing me.

I reach for my sarong and cover my bare chest.

"What the hell are you doing here?"

"I'm *from* here."

"You're from Brooklyn!" I counter, knowing that he meant
his parents are from here.

"Andreas Mihalis Crokos . . ." He reaches to shake my hand.
"But my friends call me Drew."

I smack his hand away. "How do you get Drew from
Andreas?"

"In America, I'm Andrew Michael. Here, I'm Andreas."

"Does Crokos have an English translation?"

"Crokos means lily in Greek," he says with a wink.

I think back to the flowers he sent me in Paris, but I'm still
too freaked out that a coworker has seen me naked to stay on
the thought for long. He reads me like a book.

"Don't worry, it's our little secret. Unless you want me to spread the word."

"Spread what word?"

"That you have great tits."

I'm mortified that he's seen the twins. But a woman loves to be complimented, so I'm also a bit . . . titillated.

"Not that I got a great look at them. We Greeks aren't ones to stare."

I burst out laughing. "What's up with *that*?"

"It's our national pastime. We've got three thousand years of betrayals to get over. Almost every European nation has either invaded, burned, or colonized Greece. So, forgive us if we're a little leery of foreigners. But once we decide to trust you, you've made a friend for life."

Great, that means he's not going away.

"Grab a chair already. You're blocking my sun," I say, resigning myself to the situation.

Drew settles in quickly, taking off his shirt, but thankfully leaving on his swim trunks. A lot of men are letting it all hang out, and it's not a pretty sight. Drew's body, on the other hand, is that and more. Guess one of us actually uses their gym membership. Who knew that under his Brooks Brothers shirts, Drew was hiding killer six-pack abs and hunky shoulders?

"Tell me about Morocco," I say, trying to get the image of a naked Drew doing sit-ups out of my mind.

"It was awesome. Wait till you see the tapestry I had shipped home."

All I bought this entire trip was clothes, some antiwrinkle cream you can't get in the U.S., and Ambien, for all the sleepless nights I'm going to have when I go back to work. European pharmacies are the bomb. You don't need a prescription for most drugs, and they're cheaper here than back home. But now I realize that everything I bought has a shelf life. Clothes go out of style and drugs get used up. I suddenly feel really stupid. I wish Flash had dragged me to an arts festival instead of all those damn art museums.

"How has your trip been?"

"Well, London was . . ."

I think back on my first stop. I think about Queen Charlotte, Karin, and Rita.

"London was educational."

"Educational?"

"Let's just say that it may have been a theory before, but now it's a fact. Four breasts in any relationship I'm involved in are two too many."

"Are we talking about a fat man or a woman?"

I decide to toy with him a little. "A woman. A very sexy woman. With Halle Berry boobs and a J.Lo-esque behind."

"You're killing me here, Carson. You and Halle Lopez. I would've paid good money to see that."

Who wouldn't?

"Tell me about Paris."

I think about Marie, Philippe, and Flash.

"Paris was . . . liberating."

"What's up with these one-word answers?"

"Drew, I don't want to bore you with details of my vacation."

"You could never bore me, Carson. You have a very unique way of looking at the world. Even when I don't agree with your vision, I always find it interesting."

"You'll never guess who showed up."

"Who?"

"Your boy."

He thinks for a beat. "Guy?"

"Hell, no. Flash."

"Clash showed up in Paris?"

"Bearing flowers, no less. Not as fabulous as yours, but he got an A for effort."

Drew sneers at me. "What else did he get?"

"The boot," I say.

"Is that short for the bootie?"

"Naw, I took him off the payroll."

"Wait, the last time we spoke you said everything was cool between you two?"

"And we're still cool. Only now we'll be cool from a distance. And only in the daytime."

"Can I ask what happened? I mean, he flew all the way to Paris so you two could break up?"

"He was as shocked by the turn of events as I was. It's one thing that we're not each other's soul mate, but we barely even get along. We just always seem to . . ."

"Clash?"

I give him a playful smack in the shoulder. "I hate you."

"No you don't." He smiles smugly. "So, what do you think about Greece?"

"Yesterday I was ready to go home. But today . . . I could stay forever."

"That's Greece, all right."

"When did you get here?"

"A few hours ago. I called your room and when you didn't answer, I figured you'd be here. Everybody comes here."

"What do you mean you called my room? Drew, how did you know . . . ?" I stop myself. We have the same travel agent. His travel agent.

"So this isn't an accident, us running into each other?"

"Kia, you know I come here every summer. Obviously you wanted this to happen," he teases.

At least I think he's teasing. I knew he came to Greece once a year. I didn't realize that meant at the exact same time I'd be here. On the exact same square foot of sand.

"I think it's a little weird that I came to Europe to have new experiences and I keep running into old faces."

"Maybe the point is just to see them differently."

I think on that for a beat. He may be on to something.

"Hey, Carson, whenever you want to talk, I'm happy to listen."

It takes me a minute to realize he's talking about my suspension.

"Dude, I'm on vacation here . . ."

"I know, I'm just saying that if you want to talk . . ."

"What's there to talk about, Drew? I can either walk the walk or walk out."

"When are you giving your notice?"

"What makes you so sure I'm not going the other route?"

"Carson, you're the black Evita. Walking the walk isn't your style."

"Up to now I wouldn't describe myself as a quitter, either," I say in a conversation-ending way.

I decide that I'm not going to let Drew ruin my vibe and I go back to sunning topless. After all, I'm not a quitter and I've got great tits.

Drew quickly jumps up. "I'm going for a swim."

And swim he does. Like a dolphin, fast and sleek. I remember him mentioning he played on the water polo team in college. I try to recall other personal facts about Drew. His mother makes the best baklava; she brought some by the office once when she came to town for the Christmas holidays. He broke up with his last girlfriend because she had a jealous streak bigger than her boobs. He has a cute condo in Venice Beach. He hosted a going-away party for a coworker last year. Now that I think about it, he did have some pretty cool art ... an original Bearden being my favorite.

A hush has indeed descended upon the beach. Drew is making a slow and casual stroll back to his chair and all eyes are on him. Gay men gawk, the straight ones scowl. Young women swoon, and the old ones giggle like schoolgirls as he walks past. A Greek god is in their midst and everyone knows it. Seeing his dark curly hair slicked back and his tanned skin glistening in the sun, a strange sensation rushes through me; for the second time today I'm picturing him naked. I shake the image out of my head and go back to reading my *Vogue*. Only I can't because it's in French. My eyes are once again drawn back to Drew, who has stopped to talk to a woman. Actually the two women I had first thought were black.

I watch as one of the women hands Drew what I presume is her phone number. He's been here all of thirty minutes and he's already pulling them in. In my next life I'm definitely coming back as a man. So what if they're not in touch with their feelings? Who needs feelings when you can have all the sex you want?

"Made a few friends, I see," I say to Drew upon his return.

"They wanted me to join them for dinner tonight, but I already have plans. I told them that maybe we'd meet up later at the club."

"We?"

"I'm meeting my cousin for dinner. You should join us."

Talking about dinner has made me realize the sun is beginning to go down. A moped ride in the dark seems beyond suicidal. I reach for my bikini top and Drew is all too eager to help me tie it up. To say that the moment was a little weird is like saying Michael Jackson has just had a little work done.

"Well, if I survive my moped ride home, I just might tag along. I'm already sick of the hotel's room-service menu."

"You rented a moped?"

"Yes, I—"

"Do you know how dangerous they are? People die on those things all the time." Drew scolds me like he's my father, and I don't like it.

"If they'd mentioned that in the brochure I wouldn't have done it."

I hurriedly throw the rest of my things into my bag.

Drew quickly packs his stuff up as well. "I've rented a jeep. I can put your death trap in the back."

I'm not sure what just happened here, but we're both pissed off and neither of us seems to be backing down. Despite the awkward silence, the ride home is still pleasant as I'm able to enjoy the scenery I missed on the trip up. Mykonos is like Miami Beach and the Berkshires rolled into one. It's the perfect blend of rustic and beachy. While I couldn't name any of the plants to save my life, I recognize that the vegetation is similar to that in California. I'm awestruck by how connected I feel in a place so far away from home.

Since Drew's face seems less tense than earlier, I try to make polite conversation.

"What's the deal with all these crosses scattered everywhere?"

His tense expression returns. "They're makeshift memorials wherever an accident happened or somebody died. Notice how many there are on the roadside?"

"Oh," I say, wishing I had left it alone.

We're pulling back into town now, our quiet ride almost at its merciful end.

"Which one of these morons rented you the bike?" he bellows.

"Up there on the left."

Drew swerves into the parking lot like a teenager trying to

impress his friends with his driving skills. As I hop out of the jeep, he deftly unloads the moped and follows me inside the rental office.

"I think I can handle returning the keys on my own."

Drew ignores me. The woman who laughed at my earlier request for a helmet seems very happy to see me. Almost too happy.

"Did you enjoy your ride?"

If Drew weren't being such a bugger about this, I'd tell her *Hell, no, I did not enjoy my ride. And if you were a decent person, instead of a money-grubbing whore, you'd only rent mopeds to people with a serious death wish.* Instead I smile at her.

"It was such a rush. Can't wait to do it again."

A second later she and Drew are going at it in Greek. I had no idea the boy spoke the language so fluently. And while I can't make out one word of what he's saying, the look on both their faces suggests that he's pretty much saying what I really wanted to say only didn't because I wanted to piss him off. Like me, the prosecutor in Drew is never far from the surface. Drew has gone into complete lawyer mode and he's letting her have it. He's a good lawyer. An excellent lawyer, actually. I almost feel sorry for the poor girl. Almost.

Hopping back into the jeep, it's my turn to let him have it.

"What the hell was that all about? I can fight my own battles, you know."

"If something would've happened to you I would've felt responsible. I didn't mean to yell at you and I probably shouldn't have yelled at her, but I'd have been the one to have to call your mother . . ."

That's a call nobody wants to make and I get it. It's kind of sweet that he even thought about such a thing.

"Hey, no harm, no foul. Can we just call a truce?"

"So, you don't plan to rent one again?"

"No, I just said that to—"

"Piss me off. Yes, Carson I know. You're transparent that way."

"Just when you were starting to get back on my good side . . ."

Drew pulls into the Semeli parking lot.

"Now that you've been delivered safely back at your hotel, you have no excuse not to come to dinner."

"Is your cousin cute?" I ask.

"Yeah, I guess so."

"Single?"

"Yes, why?"

"Just asking. Sure, I'll go to dinner with you. A girl needs to eat, right?"

"I'm staying at my cousin's, up the way a bit. We'll swing by around ten-thirty to pick you up."

"Ten-thirty? Why so late?"

"That's just how we Greeks like to do it, Carson. Plus, the clubs don't get going until around one."

I'm going to need a nap. I'm used to clubs closing at one, not just starting up then.

"Hey, Carson? Did you happen to bring those black stilettos that buckle at the ankle? I think you wore them to our office Christmas party last year?"

"Yes."

"Wear 'em tonight."

I smile seductively. "Your cousin likes women in heels?"

"Doesn't everybody?" he says before driving off into the sunset.

Twenty-five

Travel is fatal to prejudice, bigotry, and narrow-mindedness.

—*Mark Twain, American author*

THE JOKE IS ON ME. Drew's cousin is a her, not a him as I somehow expected. A busty blond soap-opera star who goes by the name Theodora. She's one of those balls-out, love-them-or-leave-them kind of girls. And hidden inside her laugh is the key to life.

As it often happens when hanging out with an actress, the evening has been all about her, which is probably for the best since there is a strange tension between Drew and myself—residue from our earlier spat, I can only assume.

"Andreas has told me a lot about you," she says without revealing whether the report was good or bad.

I feign indifference. "Could you pass the calamari? It's delicious."

We're dining at an upscale tapas-style bar in the center of town. It's a very chic Greek crowd with a few in-the-know tourists thrown into the mix. I can honestly say that I'm enjoying the best meal of my trip. Rich, spicy food seasoned to perfection instead of sauced to death.

Theodora passes the dish to me. "You're not dying to hear what he said?"

"Not unless you're dying to tell me," I say, delicately biting into my calamari. After watching Marie eat, I'm determined not to inhale my meals.

Theodora playfully tugs on Drew's ear. "I like her. The kind of girls I'm used to seeing you with would be champing at the bit to hear the gossip."

"She's champing at the bit; she's just too cool to let you know it."

How does he do that? How does he know what I'm thinking? It's so irritating. Why am I asking myself this? I need to be asking him.

"How do you do that? How do you know what I'm thinking?"

"I told you, you're transparent," he says casually.

"Apparently not. Theodora bought that I could give a hoot about what you think of me."

"I'm not Theodora," he chuckles slightly. "Hey, I meant to tell you this earlier, I really like your braids."

"He likes it the other way, too. In case you were wondering," Theodora adds.

I was, but no one needs to know it.

"Hey, whose side are you on?" Drew says, as the lobes of his ears turn pink.

"Yours, Andreas. Always yours," she says.

"Carson, you've got to try some of this lamb."

Before I know it Drew stuffs a piece into my mouth. As I pull back from his fork and begin chewing what is truly the juiciest cut of meat I've ever tasted, my eye catches his and for the third time today a strange sensation rushes through me. I think back to all of the meals we've eaten together over the years. And while he's always eager to share whatever he's ordered—he practically insists on it—he's never fed me before. The look on his face says he's realized the same thing. His ears turn pinker.

Theodora stubs out her cigarette. "I'm tired of sitting."

She promptly rises and hits the empty dance floor located just to the side of where we are dining. She whispers something to the DJ, and after a quick search through his apparently well-organized CD collection, he begins to play a sexy Arabic dance mix. Theodora seizes the moment, performing a one-woman cabaret act. The entire restaurant is mesmerized. Just as she planned.

Thankfully, she's worthy of the attention. Theodora performs one of the sultriest dances I've ever seen. Part soulful belly dance, part striptease (removing only her pink shawl, to reveal tanned soft shoulders that she shimmies just so).

As part of the audience-participation portion of the evening, she uses her shawl to beckon male dancers to join her by placing the scarf around their necks and pulling them onto the dance floor. Drew is her first victim. He's no Justin Timberlake, but he does manage to keep the beat. He knows to go on the two and four, not the one and the three. It's a blast watching him get his *Greek* on.

It's always a trip to see someone in their element. The person I am at the office and around my coworkers is so different from who I am at home around family and friends. I see now Drew plays that game, too. He's taken on a whole new persona while in Mykonos. Back home, Drew is somewhat of a health nut, but over drinks tonight he smoked a cigarette while waiting for our table. Okay, all three of us smoked cigarettes while waiting for our table. I notice he's wearing a beautiful silver cross around his neck that I've never seen before; it's probably always hidden under his shirt and tie. I've learned that the Greeks are very religious people. Ninety-eight percent of the country is Greek Orthodox. And now I'm watching him dance! Years of office Christmas parties and other work-sanctioned socials and he has never so much as bopped his head to the beat, let alone moved to it, but here he is auditioning to be a background dancer for P. Diddy. Maybe there's some real truth to this Andrew-in-the-States, Andreas-overseas thing.

Theodora uses her shawl to bring another man to the dance floor, releasing Drew to rejoin me. To my surprise, instead of sitting back down, he pulls me out there with him.

"You've done this before?" Drew says, impressed I've already got the Greek shoulder and hip movements down.

I realize *I've* never danced at our office parties, either. I'm always leery of dancing in front of white people. I shun all activities that feed into stereotypes about blacks. That means no eating fried chicken or watermelon at the office picnics, either.

"You should come with Theodora and me to Santorini tomorrow. It's my grandfather's name day."

"Name day?"

"Greek children are named after saints. Every year we celebrate the day set aside for our patron saint. We do that in lieu of birthdays. I promise you a good home-cooked meal and a few laughs. My family is a little nuts."

"I heard Santorini is beautiful."

"Almost as beautiful as seeing you on the beach today."

"I was wondering when you were going to bring that up." I'm unable to hide the embarrassment in my voice.

"I'm not going to lie to you. It was a thrill seeing you topless. But it was more of a thrill to see you relaxed and happy. That's how you looked to me today. Happy. And anytime a person is happy, they can't help but be beautiful."

"The sun must've melted your brain. You're being way too nice to me." I say.

"I decided today that life is too short to treat you any other way."

I impulsively kiss his right cheek. It turns beet red the second I do.

"I never did thank you properly for the lilies. First class all the way, Crokos."

"And what about Santorini?"

I smile at him. "Aw, what the hell."

"I got us tickets for the high-speed ferry leaving out tomorrow at eight A.M."

"You got us tickets already? How could you be so sure I'd say yes?"

"I wasn't sure of anything, I was just hoping. And sometimes that's enough."

I feel a tap on my shoulder. "Mind if I cut in?"

I turn around to find a dapper, silver-haired gentleman with a kind smile. Drew shoots me an *Are you okay with this?* look. I nod that I am.

"Watch out. She stepped on my foot twice," Drew says to my new dance partner.

The gentleman takes me confidently into his arms. "That's probably because you weren't holding her right."

There's nothing like being with a man who knows what he's doing.

"I think it's only fair to warn you that the last American girl I danced with, I married," the handsome devil says.

I smile genuinely at him. "I should be so lucky."

His name is Christos. He and his wife, Vivian, were married for fifty years before she passed recently from cancer. They met while on vacation in Mykonos. He lived in Athens at the time, she in Austin, Texas. Despite their many differences, not the least of which was the fact that neither spoke the other's language, their instant attraction was a bond neither could ignore. Afraid if she returned home for her things her parents would prevent her from coming back, she chose simply to start anew. He had to do the same, as his parents didn't approve of her being American and a practicing Southern Baptist. With little more than the clothes on their backs, they settled permanently in Mykonos, and started working in various restaurants, moving up from busboy and waitress to eventually owners of their own place. This place, in fact.

The dance floor is now full of people all happy to be alive and well, and living it up in Greece. At around three A.M. Christos reopens the kitchen and makes us remaining diehard partiers a late-night feast of lamb and eggs. On the house.

Without discussion, we push tables together so that we can all dine as one. Our ragtag crew consists of: a pack of young, gay, Italian designers; a lesbian couple from France; newlyweds from Ireland, Seattle, and Barcelona; a group of Australian real estate developers; three Indian sisters; the DJ, who was from Nigeria by way of London; Theodora, Drew, myself, and Christos.

That's the thing about Mykonos. It's the place where everybody comes to vacation—the capitalist, the backpacker, the adventurer, the hedonist, the city dweller, the villager. I'm not going to go so far as to say *only in Mykonos* could this group have gathered together, but I've only experienced it here.

Maybe it's the sweet Greek wine or the sweet love story Christos shared with me, but as we sit down to eat, I feel the need to say a toast.

"Here's to Christos and Vivian, for creating a place where everyone feels at home. A place where hungry souls are sated by food and good company. I sense in this room tonight a real feeling of love and acceptance, which I believe is the true lesson God sent his son here to teach us. I say this not to offend anyone here who may believe differently. It's simply what I believe and I'm secure enough in that belief that I can respect and befriend all of those who believe something else. So, here's to those of us who strive to see the world as a place full of *us* and very few of *them*."

The room is eerily quiet. The realization that all eyes are on me has me suddenly feeling very self-conscious. A jury may watch as you recite all the reasons they should send someone to jail, but they rarely look at you. Oddly enough, it's easier that way. This feels so personal and intimate.

I should've learned my lesson in Paris. I should never talk when I've had more than one drink. Somehow I always end up saying the wrong thing, or, as in this case, just the corniest thing imaginable. I catch a quick sight of Drew. And for a second there I swear I catch something in his eye as he looks back at me. And it steadies me just enough to raise my glass and finish what I started.

"To us," I say.

I didn't need a translator to understand "To us" being repeated back to me in Greek, Hindi, Gaelic, Italian, Spanish, French, and Niger-Congo.

Walt Disney was right about one thing: it is a small world after all.

Santorini

Twenty-six

Writing and travel broaden your ass if not your
mind and I like to write standing up.
         —*Ernest Hemingway, American author*

I WISH I COULD take a nap, but the early three-hour trip
from Mykonos to Santorini has me thinking about slavery. Be-
ing herded into the belly of a boat, headed off to only God
knows where (okay, so I do know where, but Santorini might
as well be Hades for all I know) reminds me of the Middle Pas-
sage. Only I'm not in leg irons and I have bathroom privileges.

Protected from the elements (a blazing sun and crashing
waves), I sit comfortably in a reclining leather seat, looking out
to sea. With my journal in hand, I'm trying to picture what the
voyage from Africa must have been like. How frightening, de-
humanizing, and painful it must have been. What if I had been
taken from my home and everything I knew, shoved into a
dark, smelly, rat-infested hull of a ship sailing for months over
rough and rocky waters? Would I have chosen to jump to my
certain death in the middle of the Atlantic or would I have
opted to stick it out and see what comes, no matter how horri-
fying the fate?

I'd like to think that I would be a jumper. It seems like such
a bold and courageous move. *In your face, white man. I'd rather
have sharks tear me in half than live the life you've planned for me.*

But then it occurs to me that if everyone had jumped I

wouldn't be here. I am a descendant of the ones who stuck it out. The ones who endured years of hardship. Humiliation. Heartache. While still an admirable and understandable decision, in many ways the ones who jumped took the easy way out. They let their fear override their faith. And in that moment, it hit me. I too was going to have to stick it out. There would be no jumping ship for me, either to the P.D's office, into private practice, or back to Paris to make purses. If my ancestors could survive the Middle Passage, I could survive Downey. Or whatever else Holden threw my way. I wasn't going to play team ball, and I wasn't going to quit. The world doesn't need another Kate Spade or, with all due respect, another Johnnie Cochran; it needs more Kia Carsons.

There are more Jamal Greenes and Terry Lewises out there I need to look out for.

There are more Belinda Maxwells out there who need the right person to convince them to do the right thing. She's not the first reluctant witness I tricked into testifying, and she won't be the last.

There are way too many Junior Simmonses out there I need to lock up. Still way too many victims of senseless crimes I need to help.

With my future settled though uncertain, I'm finally able to nap.

"WAKE UP, Carson. You're missing it!"

"Tell it to wait. I'm sleeping," I say grumpily.

"GET UP!" Drew yanks me out of my chair and pulls me onto the deck of the ship.

"This better be good. I was dreaming about . . ."

It was good. Very good. We are pulling into the port of Santorini and the quaint charm of the island blows me away. Miles and miles of whitewashed houses balanced on plunging cliffs, perched above a warm aqua sea.

"Well . . . ?" Drew asks.

"Shh. I'm still dreaming," I whisper.

I sense in his smile that he is both relieved and pleased in equal measure. As Drew and I stand in silent wonder, his hand somehow ends up in mine. And a tingle runs through me. What is going on here? I don't think coworkers are supposed to hold hands like this. In fact, I'm sure of it. And even if coworkers were allowed to hold hands, there shouldn't be tingling.

Totally freaked out, I keep my head pointed straight toward the port, but my eyes dart nervously back and forth, trying to get a read on Drew without him knowing it. My peripheral glances suggest that Drew doesn't seem to be fazed in the least that we're holding hands. Not a tingle in sight. Good, this is just a friendship thing. When his dad had a stroke and Drew was overwhelmed at work, I took over some of his cases, like any good friend would. He did the same for me when I had bunion surgery. We've broken bread together, spent countless hours at work together—surely that makes us friends. And there is absolutely nothing wrong with two friends enjoying a breathtaking view. While holding hands. And tingling.

Twenty-seven

> The one who's chasin' doesn't know where the other is taking him. And the one who's being chased doesn't know where he's going.
> —*Sam Shepard, American playwright*

"YOUR FAMILY OWNS all of this?"

Drew and I are wandering through what must be a fifty-acre olive orchard.

"Yes," Drew says sheepishly.

To his credit, Drew has always downplayed the fact that he comes from money.

"I spent so much time here during the summer as a kid, I'm glad you're getting a chance to see it."

It is a forest of leafy, tall, silvery-green, almost lyrical trees that seem to go on for miles. After arriving at his family's farm an hour ago, Drew threw a few things from his grandmother's kitchen into a basket and whisked me off for a grand tour. Theodora stayed behind to catch up on her beauty sleep. Having partied harder than the rest of us last night, she is paying the price for it now.

"For us Greeks, the olive is king."

"Don't you mean queen? Didn't Athena win the right to rule over Greece when she gave the wise gift of an olive tree?"

"Your knowledge of Greek mythology is impressive."

I flash back to my first encounter with Derrick in London and how impressed he was with my knowledge of Carnival in

Notting Hill. Women are moved by jewelry, men are moved by all roads that lead back to them.

Drew stops in front of a big tree, offering the perfect amount of shade from the blazing sun. He pulls a small blanket out from the basket and spreads it on the ground.

"Let's set up camp here."

Within minutes he's created quite a little picnic with toasted pita bread, cheese, olives, and Retsina, a Greek wine.

"Drew, since you've got me out here, you might as well tell me more."

"Because they grow on trees, olives are technically a fruit. We grow mostly *amphissis*—it's a hearty variety that yields both black and green olives as well as oil. They've got a good pit-to-pulp ratio."

"Ah, the ever crucial pit-to-pulp ratio," I tease.

"Pulp matters," he teases back.

"I should have mentioned this to you earlier, but I hate olives."

"Nice try, Carson. You order them on your pizza all the time."

"Geez, you know way too much about me."

"And here I was thinking I can't wait to find out more."

I quickly take a small bite of cheese.

"I promised my grandmother we wouldn't get too full. Unlike city folks, farmers eat dinner early. She's prepared quite a feast, so don't inhale this stuff the way you do at home."

"I'm cured of that bad habit."

"But I like watching you eat. The way you always bite into stuff when it's way too hot and then act surprised when the roof of your mouth gets burned. It's the highlight of my day."

"Watching me in physical agony is the highlight of your day?"

"No, Carson. Watching you go after what you want and damn the consequences is the highlight."

"Really? Is that how you see me? When I was in Paris you called me a chickenshit."

"There is that dichotomy about you. Some days you're a stuck-up diva and other days you're a grassroots egalitarian. Some days you're a pit bull and others a chickenshit. But let someone challenge you and you rise to the occasion every time."

"I wouldn't exactly want that on my epitaph, but now that you mention it, it sums me up rather well."

"You know, Christ spent his last moments as a free man walking through a grove similar to this one. If I could choose the last place I'd want to be on this earth, this would be it."

Taking in the tranquil majesty of these sacred trees, I could see why Drew would want to spend his final moments here.

"I'd want my last moments to be spent somewhere I've never been before. The Serengeti. Venice. Maybe even a tropical rainforest. Anywhere familiar will just stir up memories, reminding me of all I'm going to miss out on."

Drew furrows his brow. "I hate when you do that."

"Do what?"

"Just when I think I've got something all figured out, you say something that forces me to rethink it."

"You haven't figured out by now that I'm smarter than you?"

"So I learned last night. Did you mean all that stuff you said about *us* and *them*?"

"For the most part. There are some people out there who will never see me as an *us*. And it would be stupid for me to pretend otherwise. But I realize now there may be fewer of those kinds of people than I once believed."

Drew looks at me intently. "When did I stop being a *them*?"

"When I saw you dance," I joke.

"Seeing old faces in a new way isn't such a bad thing after all."

"No. I suppose not."

"Here, try one of these garlic-cured olives." He plops an olive into my mouth. "A Crokos family specialty."

"Mmm. Tangy," I say, trying to dispose of my olive pit delicately.

"Just spit it out, Carson." Drew demonstrates and his pit sails about three feet. "Some kids grow up skipping rocks. Some jump rope. We spit pits."

He spits out another. I decide to try it. My pit doesn't clear the blanket. Drew falls over laughing. I quickly devour another olive and try again. Same frickin' result. Drew is in hysterics now.

"Spitting pits is like kissing. There's an art to it. First you have to relax your lower jaw, let it hang a bit." He grabs my chin and moves my jaw around. "Now pucker your lips. Not too tight—more of a relaxed aren't-you-dying-to-kiss-me pucker."

Drew squeezes my lips together. "Then, right before you're ready to spit, take in a little air and thrust the pit out."

This time the sucker lands just shy of Drew's pit.

"Pretty good for a first-timer," he says.

"Something about the kissing references made it all click for me. I'm a really good kisser."

Drew leans in toward me. *Is he trying to . . . ?* I quickly pull back.

"That wasn't an invitation for you to kiss me."

He hands me a napkin from out of the basket. "I didn't take it as one. You've just got a little spittle on your chin."

IDIOT, I think as I wipe my chin.

"I hope you don't do that when you kiss?"

"Not usually. No," I reply.

"Let's say I *was* trying to kiss you. What would you have done?"

"Kissing is all about the moment, Drew. And the moment has passed." I take another bite of cheese. "I want to hear more about your family. How long have they been growing olives?"

"About four generations."

"That must be cool to have a family legacy like that. I mean you look at these big, magnificent trees and you can see everything your family has been and everything it will be."

"I suppose."

"Think about it, Drew. You don't ever have to worry about being unemployed. There's always a job waiting for you. It's probably why you're so cocky. You've got a trust fund on top of an olive orchard to fall back on. I've just got a spare room at my parents' house."

"You're not really thinking about caving in to Holden, are you?"

"Why do you keep bringing up work?"

"I just want to make sure somebody is going to be looking out for the underdog."

"Drew, just because you're not one, doesn't preclude you from being able to look out for them."

"I'll look out for them. Just not from the DA's office. When I found out you were suspended over the Lewis case, I charged into Holden's office—"

"What is it with you and the need to fight my battles?"

"Back in the day, Carson, they called it chivalry."

"Today they call it megalomania. Look, I don't need some white knight charging in to save the day . . ."

"I wasn't trying to save the day. I just wanted to talk to him. Before I knew it, one thing led to another and I quit."

"If anybody should quit, shouldn't it be me?"

"I should've quit two months ago. I've been offered this great job. I just wasn't ready to leave."

"But my suspension somehow helped you to be ready?"

"Holden's a dick. I don't want to work for a guy like that. The Clemency Foundation has hired me to work criminal appellate cases. You know, it's nonprofit, so the pay is shitty, but as you pointed out, that's not really an issue for me."

"Oh, to be born rich and white in America," I say.

"What do you want me to say to that, Carson? I am what I am . . ."

I come real close to cracking a Dr. Seuss green-eggs-and-ham joke, but I don't.

"That doesn't mean I can't see how unfair or unjust the world is," Drew continues. "There have been a few times when Holden told me to go for the jugular and I knew it was excessive punishment and I did it anyway. And when you didn't, well . . . the thought that you had bigger balls than me made me sick."

"I keep telling you to grow a set."

"Working with the Clemency Foundation will give me the chance to right some of the wrongs I did by following Holden's lead instead of yours."

"Flattery will get you nowhere unless you're taking Guy with you."

"Sorry, Carson. He's all yours. If it makes you feel any better, though, I'm taking Terry Lewis with me. The foundation has agreed to let me work on his appeal."

"That's a fair trade-off, I suppose."

Although I'm playing it cool, I'm genuinely moved by the gesture. Although I'm playing cool, I'm genuinely going to miss him.

Twenty-eight

*I am one of those who never knows the direction of
my journey until I have almost arrived.*
—Anna Louise Strong, American journalist

DREW'S GRANDFATHER'S name-day party isn't a celebra-
tion, it's a coronation. Eighty of his closest family and friends
are gathered to pay homage to this seventy-five-year-old man
who is not only the patriarch of a large family, but also the un-
official mayor of the entire village. But although Mihalis
Crokos is king for the day, Drew is clearly the crown prince.
Old and young women alike fight for his attention. The minute
his wineglass is empty, his grandmother gladly refills it. He
drops his fork and within seconds an aunt has handed him a
new one. A great-aunt goes so far as to wipe the garlic-yogurt
spread (*tsatsiki*) from his chin with the hem of her apron. But
the relative who fusses about him the most is Theodora. And
I'm not sure why, but it's starting to bug me.

Drew's relatives have been attentive to me, as well. Since
very few of them speak English, the attention usually comes in
the form of piling unwanted food onto my plate or smiling at
me the way people do when they're trying to be friendly but
can't find the words to express it.

Though I'm truly the outsider here, not understanding the
language or some of the cultural traditions, I'm comforted by the
realization that family gatherings are the same all over the world.

Sitting on an old, wooden love seat, watching all the goings on, it's easy to see that the Crokos clan could be the Carson family. Drunk uncles, bickering aunts, shiftless cousins. The wealthy branch of the family wishing the not-so-wealthy branch didn't drink so much. The not-so-wealthy branch wishing the wealthy branch would lighten up and have a little fun. Substitute the rack of lamb and cheese pie (*tiropita*) for a rack of ribs and some mac and cheese, and this could be my grandfather's birthday party.

"You can lose the fake smile now," Drew says, joining me on the bench.

"It's not fake, it's frozen. It's the only English your family speaks. That and 'Do you know Beyoncé?' "

Drew laughs. "My Uncle Ari thought you *were* Beyoncé."

"Hey, I thought your mom and dad would've been here."

He laughs again. "You're more bored than I thought if you're looking forward to seeing my parents. My dad is still recovering from the stroke. Not quite up to traveling just yet."

"I'll keep him in my prayers."

"Thank you. I feel bad I sort of abandoned you. I forgot how consuming my family can be."

"I get it. You're the handsome, successful relative living the glamorous city life."

"So you think I'm handsome?"

"You have your moments."

Drew flashes me a sexy grin. "Am I having one of them now?"

Yes. Yes you are, dammit, I think to myself before looking away from him.

"It's just a question, Carson. It's not a commitment."

"You've got every woman here eating out of your hand, you shouldn't need me to feed your ego any further."

Drew leans in and whispers into my ear. "The only woman here who has eaten out of my hand . . . is you."

As he pulls back his cheek softly brushes against mine. The tingle has escalated into a quiver. A tingle I could write off. Dismiss. But a quiver is a different beast altogether. Quivers have to be dealt with.

"You know you're not supposed to leave my side at these things," Theodora says, appearing from nowhere and squeezing onto the bench.

"I was just checking on Kia."

"She seems like the kind of girl who can handle herself in any situation."

"She can. But you of all people should understand how intimidating these gatherings can be," Drew says.

They share a look that makes me feel more out of place than ever.

"My mother is in rare form tonight. She's cornered me about getting married twice already."

"Is your mother related to Drew's father?"

They both snicker. Now I feel left out and stupid.

"We're not really cousins. Our grandfathers are lifelong friends. Her family lives two farms over," Drew explains.

"Our parents were afraid we might, you know, deflower each other on one of Drew's summer visits. They took it upon themselves to quell any desire by telling us we were cousins," Theodora continues.

"Clever," I say, and suddenly I'm liking her less than I did before.

Theodora grins mischievously. "One would think."

"Let's make one more round and then we'll go. Grams has a full house tonight, so I've booked us rooms at the Homeric Poems. It's one of the best hotels on the island."

Within minutes I meet ten more cousins whose names I can't pronounce and before I know it my frozen smile is back on my face. And then two things happen.

The hair moment. Any black woman who has spent a significant amount of time around white women has had the hair moment. This one was exacerbated by the fact that it took me a while to figure out what exactly Drew's twin cousins were trying to ask me. And then I got it. They wanted to feel my hair. My mortification was only intensified by the fact that it's not really my hair. It's from some poor Ethiopian girl who had to sell it in order to feed her family so bougie black women like me could fool white women into believing they weren't the only ones graced with silky, long hair. I mean, really, never once in my thirty-five years on this planet have I ever asked to feel a white girl's hair. Why do they keep asking to feel mine? Whether it was my afro in the seventies, my texturized wavy number in the eighties, or my bone-straight lye-based perm in the nineties, a white girl has had her hand in my hair. It's rude. It's wrong. It needs to stop. But I don't know how to say that in Greek, so I let the two curiosity seekers run their greasy little fingers (from the *souvlakia*, aka lamb kebabs) through my and little Galila Assafa's hair. As I stand there, feeling like an animal at the petting zoo, the second thing happens.

The kiss. I'm not quite sure who leaned into who first, but the bottom line is . . . Drew and Theodora kissed. Not a cousinly kiss. But a *kiss* kiss. A *meet me in my hotel room later* kiss. From the looks of it, a really good kiss.

And if I didn't feel like a fool before, I certainly feel like one now.

Twenty-nine

If you wish to travel far and fast, travel light. Take off all your envies, jealousies, unforgiveness, selfishness, and fears.
—*Glenn Clark, American author*

"WHAT HAS YOU SO quiet all of a sudden?"

"Nothing. I'm just tired," I say.

We're thankfully in the back of a cab headed to the hotel. All I want to do right now is take a warm bath and hit the sack.

"Come on, Carson. I know you. Something's wrong?"

"Stop saying that you know me, because you don't."

"Did one of my relatives say something insensitive? I'm sorry. I probably should've warned you some of them have never seen a black person before. Whatever was said, I'm sure they didn't mean anything by it."

I give him a defiant glare. "First off, no one in your family said anything insensitive to me. Few of them said anything to me at all. And, secondly, how do you know that if one of them had said something, they wouldn't have meant every word of it? Some people do a brilliant job of hiding who they really are until *poof!* in an instant their cover is blown. People often appear to be one way when in fact they are quite another."

We ride in silence. A full moon follows alongside of us, causing my stupidity to practically glow in the dark.

"You saw us," he says.

I say nothing. To my complete surprise, the SOB bursts out laughing.

"What is so funny?"

"You. You're jealous of Theodora!"

"I am not jealous. I do, however, find it a bit odd that you have been flirting shamelessly with me for two days and then out of nowhere you're sharing saliva with your *play* cousin."

"She's gay," he says.

"Excuse me?"

"Theodora is gay. I'm her cover. Her parents didn't want us to get together as kids, but they'd love nothing better now. Only . . ."

"She's gay?"

"Mykonos is gay central, but the rest of Greece isn't as open-minded. A lesbian soap-opera star doesn't play over here. Not to mention the fact that her parents would disown her. So, whenever I come, we pretend we're carrying on a torrid love affair. And as much as her parents want her to get married, they don't want her to move to America. They weren't that thrilled when she moved to Athens."

"So . . . what? You two plan to carry on this ruse forever?"

"It's never been an issue until now."

"And what makes now so special?"

"Our *ruse* was never meant to hurt anyone, only today it did. And I'm sorry about that. The last thing I'd ever want to do is hurt you."

"I wasn't hurt. I was just . . ."

I can't bring myself to finish the sentence, so of course, I stare at my shoes. Lime green suede thongs from Banana Republic. I'm happy to see that my bunion surgery scar has faded completely.

"Do you want to know why I didn't leave when the Foundation first approached me? I didn't like the idea of not getting to see you every day. I haven't been shamelessly flirting with you for two days; I've been doing it for three years. You've only noticed in the last two days. And right up until this moment, I thought I was in this alone."

"And what exactly is *this*?"

"This is two bozos who've wasted a lot of time playing games and dating the wrong people when the right one has been staring them in the face."

"Cassie was a total psycho. I don't know what you ever saw in her."

"She doesn't have too many kind words to say about you, either, Carson."

"Me? What could she possibly have against me?"

"She blames you for our breakup."

"That girl is crazier than I thought."

"She was pretty wacked, but she was right about you. I used to talk about you all the time, always comparing the two of you. It didn't take too long before I started resenting her for not being more like you. Independent, self-assured, yet totally, amazingly feminine."

"And you told her that?" I ask incredulously.

"Give me some credit. You know how you women are, always one step ahead of us. She accused me of being attracted to you and I denied it. But then one day I realized I didn't want her to be more like you. I just wanted you."

It's like a vacuum has just sucked all the air out of my body. "Why?"

"I don't know, Carson. I've never been with a black woman before and I thought it would look really good on my résumé. Why do you think? You're smart and funny. You give as good as you get. You're cool as an ice cube on the outside and nothing but melted butter on the inside. And you're sexy as hell."

"If I'm all that, why would I want to be with *you*?" I tease.

"Because I see you for all that you are. Because if you wanted something, anything . . . I'd tear down walls, jump a waterfall, scour the earth to give it to you. And because *I'm* sexy as hell, too."

"If you do say so yourself."

"Only because you forced me to. Look, we don't work together anymore, so there is no reason why we shouldn't go out on a date. A proper date. A get-dressed-up, take-you-to-a-fancy-place, me-and-you-only date. I could pick you up tomorrow, around eight. I've got some more family stuff to do during the day. You're welcome to come along, but I can't imagine that going to church with me and my grandmother would be a vacation highlight."

"You're going to church with your grandmother?"

"What? You thought I wore a cross around my neck because I like jewelry?"

What do I do now? He's met all my Prince Charming requirements, except of course he looks nothing like Tiki Barber: bald, black, and beautiful. I didn't exactly write that down in my journal, but I was thinking it.

Drew patiently waits for my answer.

"Make it eight-thirty," I say.

Thirty

Stop worrying about the potholes in the road and
enjoy the journey.
—*Babs Hoffman, American designer*

DESPITE A LONG, hot bath, half an Ambien, and the soft-
est sheets imaginable, I can't sleep. I call Maya for a reality
check.

"Can I really date a white boy?"

"Oh my God! The French guy caught up with you in
Greece! That's the most romantic thing I've ever heard."

"I'm talking about Drew."

"Drew? The guy you work with?"

"Yeah."

"The fine one?"

"Yeah. Wait—you think he's fine?"

"Pierce Brosnan fine," Maya says.

Another white boy who transcends the cute-for-a-white-boy
status.

"He does kind of look like Pierce Brosnan."

"And he's been feeling you for a while now."

"Maya, what are you talking about?"

"Didn't he work late every night that you worked late so he
could walk you to your car after that rapist who threatened you
escaped from lockup?"

I feel really stupid. Why didn't I see that as a move before?

"Why are you thinking about him, anyway? You're supposed to be on vacation trying to get laid."

"He's here. I ran into him on the beach. And he's asked me out on a date. A real date."

"Oh my God! That's the most romantic thing I've ever heard!"

"Maya, what is wrong with you?"

"Me? You're the one calling long distance to ask if you should go out with a sexy, smart, nice guy who also happens to be paid."

"And the fact that he's white doesn't come into play at all?"

"I always thought you didn't want to go out with him because you work together?"

"That, too."

"I know you are all into being down for the cause, but I think the time has come when we can date white boys and still check the African-American box on the census questionnaire."

"Maya, have you ever?"

"Hell, no. We don't play that in the ATL. But trust me, if Aaron doesn't propose soon, I'll be a Diana Ross, Tina Turner, Cleopatra, white-boy-dating ho. I just can't bring him home for Christmas."

"And what if he says something stupid?"

"He's a man. They always say something stupid."

"Racially stupid. Like a *you people* thing?"

"You school him. You drop-kick his ass. You forgive him. When the time comes, Kia, take your pick. But don't let that stand in the way of you finding happiness. Besides, you're more likely to say something racially insensitive than he is. We do call them white boys, after all."

"Maya, can you really see me hanging out at the Playboy Jazz Festival with a white . . . guy?"

"Yeah, because this white guy can afford a front-row box. Aaron and I will be happy to round out the foursome."

"And what are he and Aaron going to talk about?"

"What are you on—crack? The same things you two talk about. Aaron is a lawyer, too, remember?"

"And what do I do about the pink-penis thing?"

"What pink-penis thing, Kia?"

"You know how the blood rushes to their cheeks when they get excited. I'm sure the same thing happens down there. That can't be pretty."

"Okay, the fact that you're imagining what his penis looks like means the train has already left the station. So just stop living inside your head and enjoy the ride."

"Fine, it's just one date. It's no big deal."

"The big deal is that you're scared to death you like him."

"Dammit, I *do* like him. I don't know when it happened. I don't know how it happened. I just know a part of me wishes it didn't happen. I mean, having a fling with a Frenchman in France is one thing. Dating a white boy in America is something else entirely."

"If you're worried about your street credibility, don't. You're from Ladera. You did Jack and Jill. You went to Harvard Law School. You don't have any street credibility. The only reason you still get to call yourself black is that you're darker than a paper bag and you have a phat ass. Trust me, dating a white boy could only help you at this point."

"And what is that supposed to mean?"

"Come on, Kia. You're thirty-five and single. Folks already think you're gay, and in general our people aren't feeling the gay thing. They practically revoked my papers when rumor had it I experimented in grad school."

"Wait a minute. You dated a woman, but not a white boy?"

"I said it was a rumor. But for the record, a woman can always strap on a big dick."

"You think Drew has a little dick?"

"You've always claimed you weren't a size queen, now's the time to prove it."

"I hate you."

"I hate you more. Even if the dick disappoints, there is still the first kiss to look forward to. First kisses are the best. He does have lips, doesn't he?"

"We wouldn't be having this conversation if he didn't. I'm not into kissing chins. And before you ask, he has an ass. Not a big Mandingo one, but there's definitely something there to grab on to."

"Kia, that only leaves one thing—the wet dog smell."

"Why'd you have to bring that up?"

"It would've occurred to you sooner or later, and you would've used it as a reason not to go out with him. The way I see it, black men's funk isn't all that pleasant, either. We're just used to it. You can get used to the way white men smell, too. White girls did."

"Don't think I'm weird or anything, but I kinda like black men's funk. It reminds me of . . . Africa."

"Some black men's funk smells like Africa, but some of it is just straight out of Compton, and that is just nasty."

"Maya, do you think he's got some stereotypes he's trying to work his way through about black women?"

"Yeah—that we're all freaks."

"But . . . we *are* all freaks."

"Kia, it's generalizations like that that made us bed warmers for massa."

"I can't help it if all the black women I know are freaks.

You. My sister. Me, to a lesser degree than the two of you. And according to Diane, my mother . . ."

"Mine, too! I still have nightmares about the time I walked in on my parents. There is nothing sexy about seeing your mother in a thong."

"All right, so black women know how to please their men. That's a stereotype I can live with."

"Ooh, I just thought of a good white-boy stereotype. They love oral sex. You know brothas do it. Some even like it. Some are pretty good at it. But white boys love it, which means they must be really good at it."

"That makes two stereotypes I can live with."

"I still can't believe you ran into him, Kia. What are the odds?"

"Pretty high. He's Greek and he's been telling me to come here for years. He and his travel agent sort of set the whole thing up."

"Oh my God . . ."

"If you say that's the most romantic thing I ever heard . . ."

"I was going to say that I remember hearing somewhere that Greek men are really into anal sex."

"You realize that Maya Angelou—your namesake and my favorite writer of all time—was married to a Greek man?"

"We'll just let that one stereotype pass on by."

"Good idea."

"Can I just say, though, that if Drew does enter through the back door, the pink-penis thing won't be an issue because you won't have to look at it."

"I'm hanging up."

"Kia, wait . . ."

"What?"

"You don't find it a tiny bit romantic that you had to go

halfway around the world to discover that the thing you were looking for has been waiting for you at home?"

It took her a while, but Maya finally said the one thing I needed to hear.

Before hanging up I tell her, "It's the most romantic thing I ever heard."

Thirty-one

All God's children need traveling shoes.
—Maya Angelou, African-American author

HE'S GOING TO BE HERE in twenty minutes and I haven't a clue what I'm going to wear. The pressure is on since Drew has commented that I'm always so pulled together. I need to be extra pulled together tonight, but not to the point where it looks like I've spent all day trying to look that way. But what does that look like exactly? Hip-hugging jeans with an off-the-shoulder blouse or a slinky but simple white dress?

My only saving grace at this point is my hair. My talk with Maya didn't calm me as much as I had hoped. Neither did the other half of the Ambien. As I lay in bed reliving every moment Drew and I spent together over the last three years, I unwittingly undid the ends of a few braids. My attempt to rebraid them was so-so at best. So-so would never do for my first date with Drew.

Seeing that my ends had sort of a wavy, curly look, I undid them all to the base of my ears, so while the top remains plaited and orderly, the bottom is wild and sexy. It was a brilliant move to upgrade to the good hair. I'm looking like the star of my very own music video. All hair. A flawlessly made-up face. And damn near butt naked in my bra and panties (a sexy black peek-a-boo number I picked up in Paris).

Ten minutes to go and I still haven't figured out what I'm wearing. I do the only logical thing I can think of. "Eenie-meenie-miny-moe, casually cute or a little ho. Turn to the east, turn to the west. Turn to the one you love the best!" White dress it is.

Thirty minutes later I'm looking like a million bucks but feeling like a schmo. Drew hasn't arrived yet. And he's never late.

What if he's having second thoughts? Maybe his family threatened to disinherit him if he dated a black girl? What if he's come up with a slew of black-female stereotypes I didn't think of and it's just too much for him to handle? He's not coming. He's not—

There's a knock at my door. I fight my instinct to answer it quickly. He made me wait, now it's his turn. He knocks again.

"Come on, Carson. I know you're in there."

I count to ten before opening the door. "You're late."

"I'm sorry, I couldn't figure out what to wear."

I have to smile at that one.

He kisses me on the cheek and whispers in my ear, *"Eise Thea."*

"What does that mean?"

"You're a goddess."

"Thanks. You clean up pretty good yourself."

Drew's hair is slicked back, causing the gold specks in his eyes to be more mesmerizing than usual. He's rocking a fitted long-sleeve chocolate-brown shirt over cream linen tailored slacks. Definitely the right choice.

"Can you put these on for me?" Drew puts something in my hands. Cuff links. Leather, braided brown cuff links. My heart begins beating so fast I can hardly catch my breath.

"Don't look so freaked out. It's not like I'm asking you to tie my tie." He holds out his right arm to me. I slowly put the link through the buttonhole and snap it closed. He holds out his left arm. I can see his chest move. His warm breath blows past my ear.

"No matter what happens tonight, I'm going to remember that perfume."

Oh my God, he smelled me. I fasten his left cuff link, keeping my hand on his wrist longer than is necessary. I can't move. I want to move to the other side of the room. I want to move to the other side of the planet. But I can't. Kissing is all about the moment, and there will never be a more perfect one. And so I kiss him. A sweet, tender kiss. And it must be in the Carson genes, because before things get too heavy, I pull away.

Drew grabs me by the waist, gently but firmly pushing me up against the door.

"Where do you think you're going. I've waited a long time for that kiss. A kiss like that shouldn't be rushed. It should be savored."

This time he kisses me. He kisses me long and slow. His tongue exploring every inch of my mouth. Not in a frantic-search-for-a-lost-set-of-keys sort of way, but in a relaxing let's-spend-the-entire-day-roaming-through-the-park kind of way. It's the best kiss I ever had.

Thoughts go off in my head like firecrackers on the Fourth of July. Would Drew really tear down a wall for me? Yes. Yes, I think he would. Not that I've ever asked that much of him, but whenever I have asked, Drew has always come through.

How is it that Drew claims to see all that I am and I've barely seen him at all? How many other Drews have I bypassed because I was too busy staring at my shoes?

"If I don't stop kissing you now, I'm afraid the proper date I have planned will be shot to hell," Drew says, pushing himself away from me.

Kisses are like chocolate. How can a girl possibly stop herself from having one more? I step toward him, resting my body next to his.

"What exactly do you have planned for this proper date?"

"Dinner . . ."

"You and I have eaten dinner together hundreds of times."

"Dancing . . ."

"We've danced together. And not very well, since you told Christos I stepped on your toes."

"A moonlit stroll through town. Your hand firmly held in mine . . ."

"We took a moonlit cab ride through town last night."

I grab hold of his hand. "And we're holding hands now. If you really think about it, there's only one thing you and I haven't done."

"Kia, I—"

"One kiss and suddenly I'm Kia?"

"We've kissed many times before, you just weren't there to enjoy it. Carson is the coworker I could never have. Kia is the woman I always wanted."

The tingle that turned into a quiver is now a full-blown hot flash. I slowly unbutton his chocolate-brown, cuff-linked shirt.

"Yes, well, neither one of them is particularly in the mood for dinner . . ."

I unbutton two more of his buttons.

"But, if after three long years of pining after me . . ."

Two more buttons become undone.

"—you want to eat . . ."

I hit the last two.

"—dinner . . . I'm game."

"There you go again. Making me rethink my plans." He picks me up and carries me over to the bed. "Are you sure you want to do this?"

"As long as you know how."

I'm not the only one who rises to the occasion when challenged. Drew flashes a devilish grin and dives for my neck, alternating between passionate kisses and playful nibbles. The weight of his six-foot-plus frame feels good on top of me. With my dress and shoes still on, Drew removes my panties and buries his head between my legs. Ooh. La. La.

"You keep pleasing me with the appetizer, I'm not going to want the entrée."

"But you taste so sweet," he says, coming up for air.

Not quite knowing how to respond to that, I let out a bashful giggle. He does that thing that white boys do so well to me again.

After my third *O so nice* I eagerly roll on top of him.

I have a little pep talk with myself before undoing his pants. *Okay, Kia, no matter what is under here, you can handle it. He's a great guy. And he deserves a chance. So—small dick, pink dick, it doesn't matter. We're just going to hope for the best.*

"Is everything okay?" Drew asks, rightly concerned since I've brought the party to a screeching halt.

"Yeah. Did you remember to bring protection?"

He pulls out a condom from his back pocket.

"You just knew you were going to get lucky tonight, huh?"

"I was hoping, and sometimes . . ."

I finish the sentence along with him.

". . . that's enough."

As he puts on the condom, I slip off my dress.

"Wow. So much better than a picture," he says.

The look in his eye makes me melt. I bend down to slip off my heels.

"Leave them on. I know how much you like to stare at your shoes."

In one swift move, he manages to not only regain the power position but he's got my legs straight up in the air, providing me with a perfect view of my beautiful, strappy, silver three-and-a-half-inch Gucci stilettos. You gotta love a guy with those kinds of skills.

"I'll leave them on. But I'm only going to be staring at you," I say.

Cinderella may have found her Prince Charming when he slipped on her shoe. I just may have found mine when he wouldn't let me slip mine off.

Thirty-two

✈

I may not have gone where I intended to go, but I think I have ended up where I intended to be.
—*Douglas Adams, American author*

TWO DAYS LATER I kick Drew out of my bed. It's time for me to go home.

"Stay a few more days and we can fly home together," Drew begs.

"I've run out of clothes and money."

"You won't need any clothes for what I have mind, and I'll take care of all the additional expenses."

"Tempting, but I've got a life I need to get back to. Bills to pay, plants to water . . ."

"I don't want to think about that stuff right now. We should sell everything we own and become beach bums."

I give him a cocky smile. "I whipped it on you pretty good, didn't I?"

He blushes sweetly before turning quite serious. "Kia, Greece has been great but you know when we get back home things might be a little different."

Oh shit! Here it comes.

"What things exactly?"

"There are some obvious issues we need to address . . ."

I brace myself for his next comment. *Please, God, don't let him say anything stupid.*

"I love the Knicks, and you, God help me, are a Laker fan."

"Yeah, but I'm a Yankee fan from way back, and I hate the Dodgers."

He kisses me. "That's my girl."

I tingle at the sound of him calling me *his girl*.

"It is okay for me to call you that?"

"I've been called worse." I've been giving Drew a hard time for three years, why stop now? "On the serious tip though, shouldn't we discuss the whole white-black thing?"

"Haven't you figured out by now? I'm not white. I'm Greek. Discussion over."

"What's your mother going to say?" I ask.

"*When's the wedding?* Why, Kia? Are you afraid *your* mother won't approve?"

"Probably not, she's a Laker fan, too."

"I'll be sure to steer clear of any sports talk when I'm in her presence," Drew says.

"You realize that when we go places, people will stare."

"Again, I'm Greek. I'll stare back."

"Come on, Drew. It's not that simple . . ."

"Kia, I'm not naïve. I know stuff is going to pop up. But stuff pops up in every relationship. If you're committed to this, and I'm committed to this, when stuff pops up . . . we'll deal with it. It really is that simple."

"But, Drew . . ."

"Look, I've had three years to think about all the reasons why you and I shouldn't date, and I've come to the conclusion that I can handle it. Now, if you can't, then, Kia, you need to tell me now."

I'm back at a crossroads. I'm scared to death of my next step, but I feel it's the only one I can take.

"Drew, I can't do this."

I watch his chest cave in.

"What?"

"I can't . . . leave. Certainly not before we've had a proper date. You promised dinner, dancing, a moonlit stroll—and you haven't delivered on any of it. My plants are probably dead already, anyway."

"I hate you," he says.

I shoot him a smug grin. "No you don't."

"I thought you were saying no to us."

"For a second there, I almost did."

"Why didn't you?"

"Because I could travel the world inside one of your kisses. Because you wear cuff links. Because I see some of my father in you. You both make me feel like *special* was a word created just for me. Because there are two things no woman should live without: a sense of herself and a man to love."

En Route

Thirty-three

It is good to have an end to journey towards; but it
is the journey that matters in the end.
— *Ursula K. Le Guin, American author*

IT'S A QUICK FLIGHT from Santorini to Athens. It's a not-
so-quick flight from Athens to London. And a dreadful ten
hours from London home.

Drew wanted to fly back with me, but I told him that I
wanted to end my trip the way I started it—by myself. I knew
it sounded silly, but he didn't make me feel that way. In fact, I
think he was impressed.

"Aw, bollocks! The crybaby is back."

I'm thrilled to find Karin standing in the airplane doorway.
We hug like long-lost friends.

"This is so brilliant you're on my flight." She checks my
ticket. "Pardon me, Miss Business Class."

"My man upgraded my ticket for me."

"Don't say another word. I want to hear every detail. I've got
a two-day layover. We should meet for drinks and you can fill
me in."

"I'd love nothing better."

I can't wait to tell her that I made good on her challenge to
do something new in each city. I kissed a girl in London. I
stalked a stranger in Paris. I went topless in Mykonos. And,

well . . . there was Drew in Santorini. Everything I experienced with Drew in Santorini felt new. A big smile crosses my face as I think about him.

"I think I liked you better when you were a blubbering idiot," Karin teases before directing me to my seat.

Home

Thirty-four

Take only memories. Leave nothing but footprints.
—*Seattle, Suquamish Indian chief*

"KIA. Kia. Over here!"

Diane eagerly waves to get my attention as Maya rushes over to help me with my luggage.

"Welcome back."

"I can't believe you both came to get me!"

"You *are* bearing gifts, right?" Maya says.

I nod. Among the shitload of stuff I bought for myself, I bought a few things for family and friends. They'll all be pleased, I'm sure.

"You know we missed you to pieces," Maya says.

I give them both hugs. "I missed you guys, too."

Diane checks me out. "Hey, I'm the one who's supposed to be glowing."

"You are. You look great," I say staring at her bodacious ta-tas. Her stomach is still flat but her chest no longer is.

"Leo's having a field day with them," Diane says and shimmies her shoulders like a stripper. "But enough about me. You—you look great!"

I smile bashfully as Maya and Diane analyze me.

"You do look relaxed. And tan. And thin. I hate you," Maya adds as we pile into her car.

The pleasantries out of the way, the questions begin.

"So . . . was it good?" Maya asks.

"Very. And, yes, white boys do know their way around downtown."

They howl like teenage girls.

"I knew it. And the small-dick myth?" Maya asks.

"It wasn't nine inches. Probably a good seven. But it fit like a ten."

Diane claps with glee. "Was it pink?"

"Slightly."

We all laugh.

"Did he smell like a wet dog?" Maya asks.

"No. More like Gucci Envy."

"Did you guys have anal sex?"

"No, Maya! And according to Drew it's not a mandatory thing for Greek men."

"Are you in love? Because you look like you're in love," Diane says.

"I'm pleading the Fifth on that one."

Diane looks at Maya. "We'll take that as a yes."

"We're taking things slow so as not to ruin the friendship."

"God, isn't three years slow enough?" Diane asks.

"You haven't mentioned anything to Mom, have you?"

"No, Kia. I thought I'd save the guess-who's-coming-to-dinner line for you."

I pretend to laugh. "Ha, ha, ha."

"You did invite him, right?" Diane asks.

"Yep."

"Ooh, ooh, can I come?" Maya asks.

"The more the merrier."

Diane looks at me. "You really had a good time, huh?"

"I really did."

"So, what was your favorite city?"

And for the first time I don't have a quick answer. I think back on my trip. I learned I could have a good time by myself in London. I learned I could have a good time with strangers in Paris. And I learned that I could have a good time making a lover out of a friend in Greece.

But Greece wouldn't have happened if I hadn't gone to Paris. And Paris wouldn't have happened if I hadn't gone to London.

So, I give the only answer I can . . .

"The next one!"

Kia Carson's Itinerary

LONDON

Millennium Knightsbridge
   Hotel
17 Sloane Street, SW1X 9NU
tel.: 020-7235-4377

George's Portobello Fish Bar
329 Portobello Road, W10
tel.: 020-8969-7805

Buckingham Palace
Buckingham Palace Road,
   SW1
tel.: 020-7321-2233
www.royal.gov.uk

The Lamb and Flag Pub
33 Rose Street, WC2
tel.: 020-7497-9504

Pharmacy Restaurant and
   Bar
150 Notting Hill Gate, W11
tel.: 020-7221-2442

PARIS

Hotel du Louvre
Place André Malraux, 75001
   (1st arron.)
tel.: 01-44-58-38-38

Café de la Paix
12, Boulevard des Capucines
   (9th arron.)

La Grande Armée
   (Brasserie)
3, Avenue de la Grande
   Armée (16th arron.)
tel.: 01-45-00-24-77

Louvre Museum
Palais du Louvre (1st arron.)
tel.: 01-40-20-51-51

Les Deux Magots
170, Boulevard St.-Germain-
   des-Prés (6th arron.)
tel.: 01-45-48-55-25

Le Petit Opportun (Jazz
    Club)
15, Rue des Lavandières-Ste.-
    Opportune (1st arron.)
tel: 01-42-36-01-36

Homeric Poems Hotel
Fira, Santorini, 84700
tel.: 22860-24661
www.homericpoems.gr

GREECE

Semeli Hotel
Lakka Street
Mykonos, 84600
tel.: 22890-27466